HEARING HEART

HANNAH HURNARD

Tyndale House Publishers, Inc.
Wheaton, Illinois

Library of Congress Catalog Card Number 75-13966
ISBN 8423-1405-9

Published with the permission of
The Church's Ministry Among the Jews
(Olive Press), London, England

United States publications rights secured
by Tyndale House Publishers, Inc.
Wheaton, Illinois 60187

Third printing, Tyndale edition, December 1976
Printed in the United States of America

The Lord appeared unto Solomon
in a dream by night
. . . and said, "Ask, What shall I give thee?"
And Solomon said . . .
"Give unto Thy servant a Hearing Heart."
And the speech pleased the Lord,
that Solomon had asked this thing.

Marginal reading of I Kings 3:5-10

CONTENTS

PREFACE

I heard the call, "Come follow."
That was all.
Earth's joys grew dim,
My soul went after Him,
I rose and followed—
That was all.
Will you not follow,
If you hear His call?

In these progressive twentieth-century days, when man's inventiveness and scientific discoveries surpass anything known before, and his ability to exploit material forces is unparalleled, it seems as though in the realm of invisible and spiritual realities, so far from advancing to new discoveries and illumination, an extraordinary blindness has come upon him. To the majority of people nothing but the material universe is real, and anything beyond that so completely a matter of conjecture, of wishful thinking, so impossible of scientific proof, and therefore to them so utterly unreal, that they despair of ever finding a way by which they personally can experience the reality of those things which are unseen and eternal.

This strange doubt and inability to realise the spiritual realities of the eternal world is so widespread that even among professing Christians how often one hears remarks such as "God and the unseen world always seem so terribly unreal to me. I read the Bible and I do try to believe, but I never seem able to get into vital touch with God or hear His voice speaking to me personally."

"Orthodox Christianity makes absolutely no appeal to me and I seem to be losing my faith."

"I have tried being 'a Christian,' but it just doesn't seem to work, nothing happens, everything remains unreal, so I may as well give it up."

"How can I be sure of God's guidance? I never seem to get clear, unmistakable directions, let alone the startlingly unusual leadings that some other people get."

"What is this quiet time so many Christians speak about, and how do they set about keeping it?"

"I find prayer so terribly dull and difficult, and my thoughts constantly wander because the process seems so unreal. Is there any way of making prayer more vital?"

Other people say almost despairingly, "Some people must have a special mystical faculty, which makes God real to them and faith easy. I simply haven't got that faculty. There is nothing mystical about me. I am afraid I am dreadfully earthbound, and have to get along without personal, intimate communion with God."

Then there is the general attitude of such a multitude of sincere people who frankly sum up their experience in the words, "God may exist somewhere, and one hopes He does, but to me He is utterly unreal."

Such remarks as these rather bewilder earnest Christian people who have never had real doubts as to the existence of God, and have experienced a simple living faith since their earliest childhood. God is vitally real to them, but, realising that they possess no special mystical faculty, it seems strange that other people should have such difficulty in believing in realities which they and many other people have proved in their own experience to be real beyond a shadow of doubt.

Yet, as anyone knows who works on the mission field as well as in missions at home, this is the one thing which new converts find most difficult of all, namely, how to experience a personal, intimate, vital relationship and fellowship with the Lord Jesus Himself, so real that He controls and directs their lives. They depend so much upon other Christians, and lean on them for support, finding it so difficult to hear the Lord for themselves. Yet He Himself said, "My sheep hear my voice." What could be more intimate and real than that?

It is because one so often meets people in this state of doubt and unreality, and because I went through just such a miserable experience myself, that I have felt led to write this little book about the "Hearing Heart" and how God develops it in His children, sharing with you some of my personal experiences. It has been an immense joy writing it, recalling again all God's wonderful love and goodness, and seeking to share with others the secret key which unlocks joyous, personal, daily communion with the King of Love.

1
THE FIRE OF THE LORD FELL

I was brought up in an evangelical home and environment where religious beliefs were considered far and away the most important things in the world. In comparison with them nothing else really mattered, and worldliness and anything that tended to make the spiritual life and growth of the soul seem unimportant were inexorably excluded. Spiritual things and religious doctrines were obviously of such vital value to my parents that I could not fail to be impressed with a deep sense of their importance.

One could not live in my home and be carelessly indifferent to the possibility of the existence of a spiritual world. Nor could it be lightly and easily assumed that one was a Christian simply because one lived in a home where Christianity was the most absorbing topic; nor, with the example of my father and mother before me, was it possible to suppose that it was an easy thing to be a disciple of Jesus Christ, or that one could love the world and the things of the world and still be a faithful follower of the One whom this world had rejected.

I could not fail to realise that "to love the Lord their God with all their heart and their soul and their strength" was the steady aim of my parents' life, that all their joy and satisfaction was found in seeking to serve Him, and that they held everything they possessed as a trust from Him. My father's whole life seemed to be summed up in the words, "It is required in stewards that a man be found faithful." As for my mother, through all the years of her ill-health, suffering, and almost constant pain, she was so joyful a lover of the Lord Jesus that when she spoke His name her very voice changed and her face became lighted as though an inner lamp shone through the earthly vessel. "His name is as ointment poured forth, therefore do we love Him," is the verse which I most closely associate with her memory.

We hear much in these days of the unfortunate results of a Puritan upbringing, and in my own family we all experienced, as we grew to adolescence and adulthood, a most violent reaction and antagonism to this environment and outlook. But the tremendous fact remains, that the faith and life of our parents presented us with an inescapable challenge, and no child of theirs could easily drift into unbelief, or be unaffected by the things that are true and eternal.

One could and did, furiously and almost despairingly, resist the restraints and force one's way out into "freedom," but I doubt whether any child of such parents could ever remain content to be a materialist, or cease to long with inner anguish to establish personal contact with a living God. As a child of eleven years old, I did, as I hoped and believed, became "converted" by offering myself to the unseen Saviour Whose existence I did not at that time doubt.

But the outward expression of spiritual worship in which I was brought up seemed to me, from my very earliest years, dreary and depressing, and though, as a child, I felt that religion must certainly be the most important thing in the world, I simply could not find any reality or satisfaction in it. I dreaded the type of services we were obliged to attend, and Sunday was a nightmare hanging over me the whole week. But far worse was the sense of the utter unreality of everything which was unseen, above all the frightful unreality of God and the fact that the means by which we were assured we could make contact with Him just failed to work.

I prayed, but there was no answer. I went to gospel services, and was unutterably bored and depressed. I repented, but I couldn't stop doing wrong things. I read the Bible and found it the dullest and most lifeless book in the world. It conveyed absolutely nothing to my longing soul, although it was held up as the infallible Word of God, the one channel through which He chose to reveal Himself. Nothing helped. The saving power never came. The means of grace didn't work. I simply couldn't believe.

By the time I had reached the middle 'teens I could no longer believe in the existence of God, for there seemed absolutely no way of getting in touch with Him.

Earnest evangelical friends and acquaintances quoted texts at me, and used biblical expressions which conveyed nothing to my understanding, and which seemed to exasperate and disappoint me more and more. They exhorted me to believe. But how was it possible to believe something which seemed to me untrue and did not work as they claimed it should? If faith was acquiescing in doctrines, I had believed, and nothing had ever come of it. Long familiarity with the Scriptures seemed to make them meaningless.

To me the Bible remained the dullest and deadliest book in the world and going to services the worst kind of hateful boredom.

I was a miserable, morbid, self-centred person who never felt love for anyone, shut up to my own torment. Till I was nineteen I never remember feeling happy, though of course I sometimes stopped feeling unhappy. I had two hateful and tormenting handicaps. One, a horrible stammer, which whenever I tried to speak, kept me mouthing in a desperate effort to get the words out. Until I was nineteen, I never went into a shop alone, nor on to a bus or train, or anywhere where I would be obliged to speak. As a child, when we were playing in the garden alone and I was natural and unselfconscious, I could often say whole sentences, but if spoken to or asked a question, the ghastly struggles began at once.

I simply hated people, the unfeeling ones, and even the kind ones who looked away and were horribly sorry and embarrassed. At school I suffered torments and appeared a perfect fool, always saying I didn't know the answers to questions because I couldn't get the answers out. I never dared to try to ask for a further explanation of anything that I didn't understand. I was set apart from my own kind, and it is perhaps difficult for any normal person to realise how I loathed human beings.

The other handicap was, in some ways, even worse than the stammer. I was obsessed by tormenting fears, some quite ordinary ones such as many other people share, but also many abnormal ones, at least perhaps I experienced them to an abnormal degree and more or less continuously. I felt terror of the dark, terror of heights, a maddening terror of being shut in anywhere, terror of crowds, of being ill and of fainting and losing consciousness, and above all, a daily and nightly experienced horror of death.

All these I had even as a small child, and they seemed to increase as I grew older. And certainly the older I grew the more I felt the humiliation and hurt of my stammer. Morning after morning I awoke feeling that I simply could not face another day. I longed for the courage to commit suicide. Thus I grew more and more morbid and tormented and shut up to myself, unable to think of anything but my own unspeakable wretchedness. There were still times, when I was alone with nature, and with animals (who loved me and didn't ask questions or try to make me talk), when I felt almost happy. But they were only brief respites from acute wretchedness.

All this time, though I would have

given anything to believe that there was a God who could help even me, He seemed to take no notice, to pay no attention to my despairing prayers and to become more and more unreal and inaccessible. Is it any wonder that I decided that the Christian belief in a real, personal God was either due to wishful thinking, to imagination or to the blessed happiness of having a normal mind and body.

I remember standing at the window one dreary Sunday morning in the autumn, watching the wind tossing the leaves about on the lawn, and thinking with hopeless fear and despair, "That is just like life. One is altogether at the mercy of chance or fate, and there is no security or lasting happiness anywhere. At any moment one can be swept away from all that one loves, and there is no real refuge anywhere."

Why do I emphasise all this? Because in one half hour, when I was nineteen years of age, my whole life was changed, and this hateful, abnormal husk split, and fell off, and left me, not with a new physical make-up or another mental outfit but with an absolutely transformed outlook.

The way in which God made Himself real to me, and the form of response to the sense of His reality which my stammer and my fears shut me up to, I now realise are what forced me to begin to develop from the very first moment the one vital essential of the hearing heart, namely utter dependence upon Him and willingness to respond and obey. I was so utterly, not pitifully but blessedly, dependent upon Him, that I simply could not, at that stage, do anything without Him. These two agonising handicaps forced me into utter dependence upon Him, and obliged me to put the reality of His presence and help to the test all the time, even without any feeling that He was real and actually present with me.

This is what made me learn to hear His voice. But it does not alter the principle, only emphasises it in a way more normal people may not at first realise, that a hearing heart depends upon an utter willingness to obey, the whole time, in tiny details as well as big ones. In Hebrew an "obedient heart" is the same word as a "hearing heart." If one hears the voice of God, it should mean obedience, and if one obeys one will hear.

Many Christians have not infirmities and handicaps which force them to walk in their Lord's presence all the time, so they do not always realise, perhaps for a long time, that the one principle by which all God's children have to conduct their lives is the same, namely utter surrender, disregard of feelings, and a determination to act as one would if one saw Him visibly present the whole time, as the Saviour and deliverer and leader. But as things were, I was forced from the first moment into the utter dependence to which every child of God, even the strongest and most gifted, must finally come.

This is how the amazing transformation took place. In 1924, my father, the only person on earth for whom I felt real affection, because he was my only refuge, and being a stammerer himself could understand my agony, told me that he wanted to take me to the convention at Keswick. I was horrified at the very thought of being obliged to go to religious meetings all day long, shut up with a crowd of people in a tent, and at first I refused. But finally we made a bargain together. I would go with him to the convention and would attend one meeting each morning and one meeting each evening, and the rest of the day I was to be free to wander about on the hills alone.

When the convention was over we were to spend another week in Keswick, having a proper holiday. In my secret heart I thought, "If there really is a God, surely the Keswick convention is the place where He is most likely to reveal Himself to me. And if I don't find Him it will be complete confirmation that the whole thing is wishful thinking or delusion."

So I went through the whole week of the convention, attending two meetings a day, and it seemed that absolutely nothing spoke to me. God was as unreal at the end as at the beginning. The only result was that every day I seemed to grow more and more miserable. I was surrounded by thousands of people who all appeared to be happy and entirely sure of God. They seemed to be enjoying themselves enormously, and yet I was still left out in the darkness and wretchedness of unbelief. Not a single speaker uttered a word that seemed to meet my need and to lead to conviction and belief.

On Friday evening the convention ended, but on Saturday morning the great missionary meeting was held. I sat as near one of the doors as possible, as I had been told that the meeting would last about three hours, and I knew that I could never endure sitting in a crowded tent as long as that, and meant to slip out when I could bear it no longer.

However, I remained during the whole three hours, and became more and more wretched. For twelve men and women got up, one after another, and with radiant faces told us of God's transforming power which they themselves had actually seen operating in countless heathen lives. They spoke of things which they had seen and heard and their hands had handled. They had really watched God's power transforming depraved, wicked, sorrowful and despairing men and women. They knew that He was real and that His saving power was real, because they had seen it at work.

I cannot remember a word any of them said. But what no text or passage from the Bible and no earnest speaker at the convention had been able to do, those twelve missionary men and women accomplished. It is, of course, truer to say, as I now realise, that they finished the work the rest of the convention had begun. They put the final touch. For as I sat there in utter wretchedness and looked at their radiant faces, and heard the certainty in their voices, my heart said despairingly, "It must be true. There must be a God after all Who is able to save and transform even the most wretched and tormented; able and willing, apparently, to save everybody but me. Why can't I find Him?"

When the twelve missionaries had

finished, the chairman rose to his feet and asked if there were any young men and women in that great audience who had heard God calling them to the mission field. If they had responded in their hearts, would they stand up? There was a sound of rustling all over the great tent, as scores, perhaps hundreds, of young people rose to their feet. Then the chairman asked if there were any parents there who were ready to give their children to the mission field if God called them. My father rose in his place beside me, and stood with the hundreds of other parents.

That was the last straw. I struggled to my feet and hurried out of the tent. Getting on my bicycle I tore back to our lodging-house outside the town, rushed into my little room, and locking the door fell on my knees beside the bed. And at last in an extremity of despair and misery of heart I cried out aloud, "O God, if there is a God anywhere, You must make Yourself real to me. If You exist and are really what these people describe You to be, You can't leave me like this."

There was absolutely no answer, and no feeling came that He responded in any way.

I seized my Bible and held it closed in my hands, and cried again, "O God, if there is a God, Your followers say that You speak to them through the Bible. If You are real, speak to me through this book too. I am going to flap it open anywhere, and if You are real, and care about my need in any way, convince me through the page at which I open."

I flapped the Bible open and looked at it. It had opened at a chapter in I Kings.

I laughed aloud, despairingly and mockingly. "There you are, that's the sort of God You are; it is always the same. You never respond. As though there were anything to help anyone in I Kings."

And then things began to happen, though I was too despairing to realise it. For as I started to slam the Bible shut a thought came clearly into my mind. "Why not at least give Him a chance? Read the page you have opened and see what happens? Put it to the test."

So I began to read, and at the very first words on which my eyes lighted I felt a strange mental shock. For I had opened at I Kings 18 where Elijah challenged the Israelites to believe in the One true God, and declared that He would prove that He existed. And the verse where I began to read said, "How long halt ye between two opinions, if the Lord be God then follow Him."

Of course I knew the story well, but at that moment it was as though I had never read it. I felt as though I were away on Mount Carmel, standing among that great crowd of people, waiting with them to have it proved that God was real. I read how the prophets of Baal built their altar and offered their bullock, and then prayed to their supposed god to reveal himself and answer the challenge that Elijah had made, by working a miracle and causing a fire to come down from heaven. "The God that answereth by fire let Him be God." I read on, "There was neither voice nor any to answer, nor any that regarded." I almost sobbed as I read. That had been exactly my experience all my life long, beseeching and calling to a God who did not answer or respond. What would happen next?

And I read that towards sunset Elijah said to all the people, "Come near unto me. And all the people came near unto him. And Elijah repaired the altar of the Lord which was broken down." And then he laid on it the sacrifice.

The altar—the place of sacrifice! Ah, that was it! A thrill of terror went through me. For these words suddenly gripped my mind with a pang of agony. Yes, here it was—the thing I had always subconsciously dreaded. Before God revealed Himself, He demanded a sacrifice. Christians said that Christ Himself was the sacrifice, the substitute for our sacrifice. But in that bitter moment I knew that there was no escape from the truth. I too, like the men of old, must lay on the altar a sacrifice.

Even as a child, in the strictly evangelical home in which I had been brought up, this thought had always haunted me. If only one could find God without Jesus Christ. God Himself sometimes sounded like a kind and good father, but Jesus was terrible. He said, "No one can come to the Father but by Me," and that all that come to Him must take up the cross as He did, putting self to death in order to be able to follow Him, and that they must sell all that they have, or they cannot be His disciples.

Here it was.

The place of terror and dread. The place of sacrifice. The place where I must yield myself utterly to One who would, somehow, in some agonising way, put me to the horror of crucifixion. And the thought came to me vividly and clearly, in a dreadful flash of mental enlightenment, "What this unknown God is going to demand before He makes Himself real, is that I yield to Him my stammering tongue, and agree to be His witness and messenger."

I can only say that that was the thought that came to me with terrible torturing clarity. All the time then this was why He had never made Himself real. He was waiting until I would agree to give Him my stammering tongue and tell Him that He could use it in any way that He chose.

In imagination I saw myself opening and shutting my mouth in a crowded hall with a sea of embarrassed faces before me, unable to utter a single word. And I cried out in almost frenzied dismay, "No, I can't do that. I would rather go straight to hell. If I can't know God any other way, I won't know Him at all." And then the dreadful realisation swept over me, "But it's as though I am in hell already. Oh, I need Him. I need Him. No one else can help me."

It looked utterly impossible. I did not believe that I could yield. It was dreadful to say that deliverance was free and all of grace, and then to demand such a price as this. He was still so utterly unreal. I could feel nothing but agony and despair.

How He managed it I still

cannot understand, but at last there came a moment when I cried out again, "O God, if there is a God, if you will make yourself real to me, I will yield my stammering mouth." And I looked down at the Bible and read verse 38. "Then the fire of the Lord fell and consumed the burnt sacrifice, and licked up the dust and the stones and the water in the trench. And when all the people saw it, they fell on their faces and said, "The Lord He is God. The Lord He is God."

And at that moment I became as sure that He stood there beside me as if I had seen Him with my eyes. I felt nothing. I saw nothing. But into my lonely, dark, tormented heart, there flooded like a burst of sunlight, the realisation which has never left me all these twenty-six years. Jesus is real. He is here. He loves me, even me. After all, He loves me, and has come to tell me that He wants me, that He will use me, even with my stammering, use me whom nobody else wants, who am so handicapped that I supposed I could never become of use to anyone. He wants me. He is real.

I was crying like a baby, but something miraculous had happened. The old fettering and tormenting husk had cracked and fallen off. In one sense an utterly new girl was kneeling on the floor, a girl who for the first time in her life felt joy, felt secure, felt able to laugh, could have clapped her hands and danced for sheer ecstasy of heart.

He is real: He is here: He loves me: He actually loves me. I am perfectly safe.

I went into

that room at 1 p.m. on July 26th, 1924, and I came out of it at 1:30 p.m. after that half hour of agony, completely transformed. Life was utterly different and radiant from that hour. I do not mean that my whole nature was changed and self-absorption went. The new spiritual life of Christ develops slowly and only gradually changes the old temperament and character. Outwardly everything was exactly the same.

My fearful nature was still there. My stammer was still there. My dread of people was still there; and so was my complete ignorance of how to begin thinking about others and considering their interests. I was still the old Hannah, but in some miraculous and mysterious way I had been lifted into a completely new mental and spiritual environment, out of the border-land of outer darkness, into the light and glory of heaven. It was as though a miserable, stunted plant had suddenly been transplanted from a tiny flowerpot, into a sunny, richly fertilised flowerbed. I was lifted out of the dreadful isolation of self-imprisonment and set down in the love of God.

Tersteegen gives us a most beautiful description of his own conversion. He says that until then he had been like a little frightened child crying all alone in a dark room. And suddenly it was as though the door opened, and light came streaming in, and there were loving, reassuring faces bending over him, and strong arms lifting him up into a place of security. That exactly describes my own experience. Or it was like being lifted out of a winter land of ice and desolation, to be set down in a summer land of light and flowers and bird-song.

When the bell rang for lunch, I went downstairs like one in a dream, but as soon as the meal was over, I hurried back to my room again and opened my Bible, that old "dull, dreary book" which had always so depressed me, and which had suddenly come alive, exploding like dynamite when the fuse is lighted, smashing to pieces the gates of my hateful dungeon. Now I felt a continual thirst to be reading it, to see what God, the real God, would say to me through it. It became to me an infinitely precious possession, and I began from that very first day to carry it about with me all the time, so that I could keep opening it and reading and learning from it.

Now I opened it for the second time only, with hungry excitement, and prayed "Lord speak to me again." And the verse He turned me to, in His tenderness and gentle understanding of my childishly haphazard way of looking for His message, was this: "My grace is sufficient for thee, for my strength is made perfect in weakness" (II Cor. 12:9)

That precious promise and assurance sank into my thankful heart and became the key or foundation verse of my life. He wanted weakness—who so weak as I? He promised that His grace, that wonderful, transforming grace into which I had just been lifted, would prove sufficient all the time. Up till then the name which had best described my nature was Bunyan's "Miss Much Afraid." But now He made my own name Hannah, which is the Hebrew word for grace, my real, true name. Every time anyone called me Hannah, I could think, "His grace is really sufficient for me, and His strength is made perfect in my weakness."

I remember weeping and laughing at the same time for pure joy, I who up till then had known so little of laughter. Then I went to tell my father what had happened, and that I was sure that God, the God who at last had made Himself real to me, wanted me to be His messenger, and I had promised that I would be, and therefore I must go to a Bible College and train as a missionary. I do not think that anything else in the world could have given my father so much joy. We knelt down together and with my stammering tongue I thanked the Lord Jesus, for the first time in front of someone else, for the wonder of His love which wanted even me.

So the new life of awed, amazed joy and perfect security began. I remember asking myself that first day, "Can this extraordinary joy and assurance really last a whole week? Will it still be true next Saturday, or will everything have faded away completely?" That was over a quarter of a century ago, and it has not only lasted but how immeasurably it has deepened! For then I had no experience to confirm and strengthen the assurance, but now I have had twenty-six years in which to experience over and over again that He has never been known to fail those that put their trust in Him.

From the very first moment that He made Himself real to me, He led me to this decision: "If He is really here as His word says, then I shall speak to Him and ask Him questions, and act in every way as I would if I could actually see Him." Even at times when I feel no assurance or begin to doubt, I will still act and obey as though I see Him visibly present. And so I did. And I found that I had to keep on putting the reality of His presence to the test.

I nearly always felt as though the whole experience were not true and had been a dream or delusion. But every time I spoke to Him, and acted as I would have done if I had really seen Him, it worked. And though at first every obedience looked impossible and I felt sick with fright as I tried to stammer out to my friends and family of the new faith that had come to me, the same overwhelming sense of the reality of His presence always followed every act of obedience.

When we were alone together I never spoke to Him in anything but everyday language, with complete naturalness and no artificial phraseology. As I walked on the hills or by the lake with my precious little testament in my hand I never dreamt of using formal language or of expecting His words to come to me (apart from the Bible itself) in anything but my own everyday vocabulary. It was obvious He used one's own mental faculties to receive the thoughts He wanted to give, and it was therefore natural to suppose that He would use the sort of vocabulary I had acquired in which to clothe those thoughts.

In other words, just as He wanted to use my mouth, so He wanted to use my mental faculties, and very quickly I came to realise that those faculties, and my mouth, must be wholly dedicated to His use and kept cleansed from all defilement. I realised this in theory from the beginning. But how many, many years it was before I experienced this in continual practice. Sometimes all my faculties were wholly yielded to the Lord and, at that time, I could hear His voice. But more often I used them just as I wanted, and then the old selfish, unclean thoughts came flooding in again.

2
GIANTS IN THE WAY

All things are possible to him
That can on Jesu's name believe
Lord, I no more Thy name blaspheme,
Thy word I lovingly receive.
I can, I do believe in Thee,
All things are possible to me.

This Saviour, Who had revealed Himself in such a wonderful way, went on to lead me and teach me also in the most gentle and loving manner possible. On the Sunday following that amazing Saturday at Keswick, I heard the Marechale preach in the little Methodist chapel. With what joyous, expectant alacrity I went to that meeting, so unlike the dreary distaste I had always felt for Sunday worship. The building was crowded to capacity, people looking in through the windows, clinging to the sills and balancing on ledges.

The Marechale took as her subject David and the giant Goliath, and spoke of the giants which we too were likely to meet in the way as we followed Christ. For me, this was the perfect message. Surely no pilgrim ever set out to follow the Lord with a more trembling and fearful heart than I did. Looking shrinkingly towards the future, it seemed to me that, handicapped as I was, every step of the way before me must cost pain and tears and humiliation. As far as feelings were concerned, it felt absolutely impossible, as though already a giant straddled right across the way threateningly, and I should have to turn back.

But as I listened again to that old, extraordinarily inspiring story, told in the Marechale's own dramatic and vivid fashion, of the boy who faced the giant before him with nothing but the five pebbles out of the brook (the simple promises of God) and who, as he went forward to meet the giant, was able to slay him at the first throw, a flood of hope and encouragement swept into my heart. I leant forward in my seat, almost breathlessly drinking in her words, when suddenly the Marechale bent forward over the rail of the platform and seemed to point her long slender finger straight at me. Pausing in her address she said, "You, too, are afraid of some giant in the way before you. Never fear. Meet him in the name and strength of the God of David, and though you feel like a grasshopper in comparison with him, he will fall to the ground before you."

That was the message I took with me from Keswick, as I started out haltingly and "much afraid" to follow my Lord, but, immediately, I found that Keswick had given me much more than I had realised during that long miserable week when no one seemed able to meet my need. For it was those days at the convention, little as I had realised it at the time, which shaped, very largely, my whole Christian life. Every evening of that week I had been at the meetings for young people conducted by the Rev. Stuart Holden and Mr. Clarence Foster, and night after night they had tried to emphasise for us the vital principles of Christian growth, and all these things I now remembered, although they had seemed of so little help to me at the time.

They warned us to keep separate from everything which would tend to draw us back into the old life of unbelief. They urged us to witness to others, for if we were not willing to share in this way, we would soon find that we had nothing left to share, and everything would become unreal to us again. And they underlined the immense importance of daily, thoughtful, prayerful study of the Bible.

But the thing which they emphasised most of all was the need for an early morning quiet time every day, or as they called it "the morning watch." We were urged to rise at least three quarters of an hour earlier every morning, in order to meet the Lord and listen to Him. This was stressed as the most important essential of all, and we were told that nearly all the people who acknowledged that they had slipped back into indifference or unreality in spiritual things, confessed that it began with neglect of the daily quiet time, and failure to give the Lord an opportunity to speak to them alone and to train them in hearing His voice.

It was Clarence Foster who read out to us some of the notes which he had received from young people at the convention, confessing what a struggle it was for them to get up early in the morning to keep their quiet time, and some of the ingenious ways they had contrived for making themselves wake up. But it was Clarence Foster's own suggestion, which, now that the time had come to leave the convention, came back to my memory most clearly and set the key-note for my life. In urging upon us the vital necessity for meeting our Lord for at least one personal interview each day, he put it before us in this way.

"You are all young people, and you all sleep soundly and heartily. You find it frightfully difficult to leave your beds in the morning. That is, all of you except those who are lovers and who make a tryst to meet your loved one early every morning before breakfast and before the Convention meetings begin. You are never late at that tryst, and it is never really difficult for you to get up early for such a meeting. Will you not look on your Lord as the great Lover, and go to meet Him in the same spirit? And look upon the Bible as His love-letter, and read it over and over again with the joy and attention with which you read your earthly lover's letters."

Remember I was just nineteen. My lonely, loveless heart had at last found a centre on which to rest with absolute thankful security. I loved for the first time in my life. I had, in actual fact, fallen in love, in response to the love and tenderness and understanding gentleness of the Lord. Morbid, abnormal people, and people who stammer, possibly, may not have human lovers.

Well, that no longer mattered in the least. I had Him, the Lord of love, and to the limit of my naturally unaffectionate, cold heart, I did love Him. And in that spirit I did begin rising early every morning in order to go out to meet Him, wandering in the woods, or by the lakeside, with my Bible in hand, reading and pondering and always asking questions. That Book was His Word to me. By studying it I would learn what He wanted me to do, and would find as I took hold of its promises and assurances, that it mediated His enabling grace to me.

I never felt Him present, and there was always a constant inner suggestion or pull-back, "He isn't real after all." But I learned to take no notice of that and say, "O Lord, I know you are real. Let me speak to you as though I saw you. Speak to me and make me understand the meaning of this portion which I am reading. What do you want to teach me through it? What do you want me to do afterwards as a result of reading it?"

Then as I turned to the Bible and read it again it seemed as though my thoughts in some way received new illumination, my thinking became clearer, my understanding deeper than before. He used my ordinary mental faculties and encouraged me to ask questions all the time. There was absolutely nothing possible about it, no waiting for thoughts to come to me out of the blue. But He seemed to clarify my thoughts as I expressed my questions in words or in writing, and enabled me to think the answers He wanted me to receive.

Often of course

it was just my own thoughts that came to me as I pondered on the subject I was reading each day, but I quickly became able to recognise His answers to my questions, for those thoughts came with a clarity and a kind of illumination which my own conclusions lacked. It was as though all of a sudden something clicked in my mind. "Ah that's it; that is what He wants me to understand. That's what He wants me to do. So that is the meaning of this passage; why did I never see it before?" This of course gradually developed as I got up day after day for my quiet times.

What a struggle it was to wrench myself out of bed instead of enjoying that dreamy, snug half hour before a late as possible rising, and before all the difficulties and struggles of the day began. For several years I felt desperately that it would never become easy to get up in the morning. It was a new battle every day. But up I got nevertheless, for I knew that everything depended on it. I knew from the word "go" that those early morning quiet times during which His presence became a living reality again, day by day, were for me absolutely vital. Everything depended upon them, for without Him I could do nothing.

All the time there was the constant suggestion of my senses and my fears that He was not real after all. Nothing but a personal interview with Him could renew the reality and enable me to continue obeying, by beginning to confess with my stammering tongue to my acquaintances, that I now believed in Him, by attempting to go into shops alone and on buses, and beginning to do things for myself.

It was when it came down to those ordinary, everyday, but impossible-looking acts of obedience, that I always felt that He could not be real, and that the whole thing was an illusion of my imagination. For at those times I never felt Him near. It was only as I set out to obey, and after obedience, that the sense of reality and joy returned. He always enabled me to do the things that I dreaded, after He had first made me willing, and though it cost much pain and inner struggle, the joy which followed obedience outweighed everything else.

So two and a half months passed, and in the autumn the time came for me to go to Ridgelands Bible College. I was still stammering, but not so badly as before, and I had even managed, after a great struggle, to pray very briefly in public.

I decided that I must go alone in the train and on the underground, though I had never done such a thing before, even though I was then nearly twenty years of age. I was bitterly certain that I would never be able to pronounce the name "Wimbledon" at the ticket office, nor "Ridgelands, Ridgway," to the taxi-driver, "W" and "R" being particularly agonising consonants. Of course, I might have written each name on a slip of paper and passed it to the ticket collector and the taxi-driver, but that not only looked like giving in but was almost equally humiliating. I prayed and leant on the Lord and said in my heart, "If it's what You want, Lord, I don't really mind the humiliation, though it hurts sickeningly," and took a deep breath and stuttered out Wimbledon surprisingly quickly, and the same in the taxi.

Everybody was amazingly kind at the Bible School, and the Christian fellowship made me radiantly happy. There was no need to talk much. I enjoyed the lectures and did not have to answer questions, and new students were not appointed much practical work during the first weeks, while they were learning methods and being prepared.

But there was one event which loomed up like a nightmare before me. This was speaker's class, which was conducted every Thursday morning. The principal always gave a short lecture first, full of hints and teaching for speakers, and then four students in turn delivered short addresses before the assembled staff and students, after which the addresses were briefly criticised or commended by the principal; faults to avoid were commented on and nervous mannerisms were pointed out, and the assembled students had to decide whether they had found the address interesting or dull, helpful or empty, and well or awkwardly expressed.

Obviously this was a rather nerve-racking ordeal for even the most fluent students, and to a person who stammered and who had been sheltered from the need to make any sort of effort in public, it looked appalling. And to my unutterable horror I found that my name was down on the list for the second or third Thursday in the term. Afterwards, of course, I realised that this was all in the loving ordering of my Lord, for it would have been unbearable to have the ordeal hanging over me all the term.

But when I first made the appalling discovery that in one week's time I must address the assembled staff and students, I felt that it was grotesquely impossible and that I ought never to have come.

I cringed with fear and then rushed to my cubicle, and going to the drawer, took out my purse, with the intention to taking a ticket for home at once. Standing there with my purse in my hand, and looking at my panic-stricken face in the mirror, the thought came to me with crystal clearness, "You can't do it, of course, Hannah, but isn't this just what you promised Me you would attempt to do for My sake? Won't you trust Me in this matter? Won't you put me to the test on Thursday and see whether I fail you or not? You can't but I can. And with Me you can do all things. I told you at Keswick, 'My grace is sufficient for you, for My strength is made perfect in weakness.' Now prove it." I put the purse back in the drawer, and said, "Yes, Lord," and then sobbed with terror.

When the dreadful morning came I felt so physically ill with fright it seemed as though one of my special obsessions of fear would occur and I would drop dead with a heart attack. But the amazing thing was that I actually went to that class and sat there with the other students instead of running away.

The moment came when the principal finished her lecture, and I, the first of the four students, had to get up, leave my seat, and mount the platform. At that moment God seemed as remote and unreal as though He existed nowhere. The past three months seemed to have been a ridiculous delusion. But in some extraordinary way the will-power was given to me to do what I have had to do countless times since then, namely, to ignore the dreadful physical feelings of almost paralysing fear, and act as though I were not afraid.

I walked to the platform, stepped up on to it, and turned round and faced my audience. There they were, just as I had seen them in imagination, in my little room at Keswick, a sea of faces, all looking uncomfortable and sorry for my misery. But as I stood there, actually on the platform, preparing to obey the Lord, the thing that seemed a miracle actually happened. Every particle of fear fled. The moment I opened my mouth to obey the Lord, it was as though He almost visibly stood beside me, and was speaking for me. I opened my mouth and for the first time in my life I found myself speaking without a trace of stammer or even hesitation, talking just like everyone else. I said, "My text is, 'My grace is sufficient for thee, for My strength is made perfect in weakness.'"

The little address had, of course, been prepared beforehand, with its three orthodox divisions and headings, just as we had been taught in the first lectures. But as I came to the end of it, I looked out at all those faces which were now smiling at me with astonished and relieved encouragement and said, "You see how true it is, how wonderful our Lord is; how safe it is to trust Him. No matter how weak we are, He can do wonders, just like making me speak without stammering for the first time in my life."

When the class was over one of the tutors came to me and said "Hannah, I am sure God has given you a gift for speaking. Consecrate it to Him and no matter how nervous or afraid you feel, determine never to say no when you are asked to speak at meetings." And then and there I made Him that promise, "Lord I will never say no when I am asked to witness for Thee or give an address, or take a meeting. But I will never use my mouth for any sort of public speaking, unless it is witnessing for Thee."

From that time the stammer practically disappeared, wholly when I was preaching, but the tendency still remained in ordinary conversation, especially when I was tired or over-strained. But the feeling that I should be unable to speak never left me. Every time I got up to speak before others I felt it was impossible. And for years all the wretched physical sensations and accompaniments of fear remained. But strangely enough this was never apparent, and people often said to me, "Don't you ever feel nervous when you are speaking in public? You seem to do it so easily."

To me the fact that all of a sudden I began to speak without stammering never seemed as marvellous as the extraordinary fact that the God who had been so unreal and was still invisible, Whose voice I could not hear, and Whose presence supporting me I could not see, had yet been able, without any visible or material means of persuasion, to make me willing to attempt a thing which nothing on earth would have persuaded me to do otherwise. That did seem a miracle, the most joyful and amazing miracle in the world. He was so real, so certainly there, He could enable me to trust Him and to take risks, without giving me any visible assurance.

Now I began a completely new existence. I learned to visit from house to house in the slums of London, to preach in gospel halls, and in a medical mission, to speak at lunch-hour meetings in factories, to visit the sick in hospital, and to stand on a box or chair on Wimbledon Common and witness in the open air, acting and behaving just like all the other students. It seemed impossible that it could really be I myself doing all these extraordinary things instead of shrinking away from strangers and being afraid to board a bus. Often during those first years, when I sat in a train or bus on my way to take a meeting somewhere, I found myself wondering, "Can this really be you, Hannah, willing to do it, still able to go on and finding He never fails?"

But obedience was always tested to the hilt, it never became easy, and the inner suggestion invariably presented itself, that one day the power would fail and He would let me down. I learned that I must never pay any attention to these fears and doubts, but always go forward, acting as though I could actually see Him beside me, see His understanding smile, and hear His reassuring voice saying, "My grace is sufficient for Thee, for My strength is made perfect in weakness."

In one way I lived a double existence in

those early years for I was constantly attacked by the old fears and misgivings and wretched physical feelings, and nearly every day there were agonising inner struggles before any act of obedience to some new call of His. And yet, on the other hand, every obedience was followed by a flood of amazing joy impossible to describe. It always seemed a marvel that He enabled me to keep going forward and not to turn back. But gradually I began to discover that, in actual fact, He never gave me a chance to turn back or to say no I can't or I won't.

For these very handicaps which had threatened to wreck my whole life were now my greatest safeguards and blessings. His love, which had been determined not to leave me in my misery, was just as determined that I should not turn back to it again. For every time I turned away from Him, even for an hour, I found I was turning towards the old dreadful darkness. All my fears revived and all the old sense that He was unreal came rushing back upon me like a pack of hounds, and from that nightmare existence, which now that I have tasted heaven did indeed seem like outer darkness, I was forced to turn and rush to the Lord again for protection. It was often terribly hard to keep on following, but far harder to turn back and face the loneliness and misery from which He had saved me.

So I learnt, in this perhaps abnormal way, the one vital principle of the hearing heart, namely, that one must keep in closest contact with Him and be willing to obey at any cost. For His Love had shut me up to these two alternatives, I must either follow Him no matter what He asked me to do, or turn back to the old nightmare existence of being imprisoned in myself.

Thus I gradually came to realise that these two handicaps which had so tormented me were, in reality, two special love gifts from the Lord. They were the two sharp nails which nailed me to Him, so that I could never want or dare to go on my own again.

During the past twenty-six years, I have quite often met Christians who believe in faith healing, who have said to me that God never wills that any of His children should suffer from any physical weakness or infirmity. They have asked me why I did not pray to the Lord to take away the remaining tendency to stammer in ordinary conversation, especially when tired. But over and over again during the first years of my Christian experience I did beseech the Lord in tears and pain, that He would do that very thing. But He gave to me the same message that He had given to Paul when he begged to have his thorn in the flesh removed, "My grace is sufficient for thee, for My strength is made perfect in weakness."

He made me realise that this tendency kept me utterly dependent on Him and was a continual opportunity for Him to display His power. And when I understood that, I could never ask for its removal again. Does a woman offer back to her husband the love gifts he gave her when he first told her of his love?

I do confess that there have been times during the years when I have knelt before Him in bitterness of spirit, like my namesake of old, and cried out, "Lord, hasn't the time come when the last trace of this infirmity could be removed? Haven't I learnt yet to be so dependent on Thee that I can do without it? But don't take it from me if it makes me less dependent on Thee. Only never let me allow it to hinder me in Thy work, or use it as an excuse for neglecting anything Thou dost want me to do." And always He has said, "Keep my love gift. I chose it for you myself. It is the thing through which I bless you most of all." And one of the things I look forward to when I see Him face to face is to thank Him for this precious thorn.

Fears, of course, are quite a different matter. The sooner every fear is got rid of and turned into faith the better. I learnt this as a very young Christian through reading a little article in a C.A.W.G. magazine; an article written for nervous, worried and anxious people. It said something like this: never mind if temperamentally you are very fearful and prone to anxieties and worries, for that gives you a wonderful opportunity to practise more faith than other people. Turn every fear into faith at once, and look what an advantage you have! Endless opportunities of putting God's gracious promises to the test and of trusting Him.

This new, lovely idea gripped my heart and gave me a completely new attitude towards my fears. They could all be turned into faith. It seemed to me that this gave me almost an unfair advantage over normal, healthy people. For people who have more opportunites than others for practising faith ought surely to be able to develop a strong faith more quickly than others.

I shall never forget the amazed and awed feeling that came over me when I was still a student at Ridgelands, when one of the other students said to me, "I almost envy you your stammer, Hannah, it seems to keep you so close to Him, and make Him so real to you. Whereas I am always slipping away into unreality, and trying to manage without Him." It had never occurred to me that anyone observing what I felt to be my awful handicaps should think them something to be envied.

But, of course, really, we all start equally handicapped, though our handicaps differ in kind. Capable, self-confident people with wisdom and much common sense have to learn faith too, and to keep turning their own talents and abilities into utter dependence upon God. Natural strength is often as great a handicap as natural weakness, both must be utterly yielded to the Lord.

But it was when I was introduced to Frank Boreham's books that I really made the discovery of the blessedness into which my fearful nature could lead me. Surely Frank Boreham is the prince of writers for those who are fearful of heart. One day I came across his sermon on scarecrows, and that simply amplified and glorified the principal of turning fear into faith, and it has inspired me to go forward along some frightening-looking path more times than I can number.

He says, "As with the virgins in the parable, so with the birds of the field, there are two kinds, the wise and the foolish. A wise bird knows that a scarecrow is simply an advertisement. It announces in the most forceful and picturesque way that in the garden which it does its best to adorn, some very juicy and delicious fruit is to be had for the picking. There are scarecrows in all the best gardens. Every thoughtful bird learns in time to regard a scarecrow as an invitation to a banquet. He feels as a hungry man feels when he hears the dinner bell ring, and swoops down upon the delicacies to which the scarecrow calls him. If I am wise I too shall treat the scarecrow as though it were a dinner bell . . . . Every giant in the way which makes me feel like a grasshopper is only a scarecrow beckoning me to God's richest blessings. Faith is a bird which loves to perch on scarecrows. She knows that there are scarecrows wherever there are strawberries. All our fears are groundless."

So life for me became more and more transformed. But I was so taken up with the new joy and liberty which had been given me that I did not at first realise how much else there was for me to be liberated from beside my fears and my stammer. I was very little changed in matters of temper, irritability and selfishness. I felt myself so astonishingly transformed within that it never occurred to me that there were others who would doubt the reality of what had happened.

One evening, however, I tried to tell one of my sisters, who was home during the university vacation, a little of the amazing thing that had happened to me, and to urge her to seek for the same joyful experience. She listened for a minute or two and then said deliberately, "It is people like you, Hannah, who put me off being a Christian. You may be happier yourself, but I can't see that you are any less selfish, nor as far as I can judge any easier to live with. You go about impertinently preaching at everybody, and remaining just as determined to have your own way in everything as you were before."

I was completely taken aback by this counter-attack, and horribly confounded, for I realised how much truth there was in it. At last I blurted out, "But you know the Lord Jesus isn't a bit like me. Don't look at what I am. He is the One who is perfect. He only took me in hand such a short time ago. In the end, you know, He has promised to make all His followers, even me, like Himself, and to perfect that which concerns us."

But it is a long painfully slow job, having the roots of selfishness and bad temper and irritability and laziness, and all the other sins and defects so natural to human nature, put to death. A much more difficult job than being delivered from infirmities and handicaps. But His endless, patient love never gives up. It will never fail. How skilful He is. Nobody teaches as He does.

3
I AM READY

> Got any rivers uncrossable?
> Got any mountains you can't tunnel through?
> We specialise in the frankly impossible,
> Doing the things that no man can do.

When I had finished my two years at Ridgelands Training College I joined The Friends Evangelistic Band for further training in work that would prepare me for the mission field. The Band was an interdenominational faith mission doing evangelistic work in the villages of England and Ireland. If the two years at Ridgelands had been radiantly happy and had introduced me into a entirely new environment, what can I say about the four years in the Band? I had never supposed that it was possible for anyone to enjoy life so much or live so in the atmosphere of heaven.

Of course I know that there were many times of difficulty and battle and often of failure, but, looking back, memory only recalls those years as shining with golden light like an early summer morning, sparkling with dew and full of singing birds. It is true that the years in Palestine have been still happier as union and fellowhip with the Lord have deepened with the passing of time, but perhaps it was because the contrast was so great between the new joy and the years of misery and loneliness which had preceded my conversion that that time seems to have been full of an almost indescribable gaiety and carefree light-heartedness and delight in Christian work. The hymn we so often sang in those days sums it up:

> In the glad morning of my day,
> My life to give, my vows to pay,
> With no reserve and no delay,
> Lord of my life I come.
>
> Just as I am, young, strong and free,
> To be the best that I can be,
> For truth and righteousness and Thee,
> Lord of my life I come.

The motto of the Band at that time was "Ready for Anything." Ready for anything the Lord asked us to attempt and ready to go anywhere He sent us. I was twenty-one when I joined them, and rather embarrassed and shocked my relatives by traveling about the country in a caravan, holding open air meetings and missions in village after village. When I first joined the Band it possessed only two horse caravans and one motor van, and there were about twenty workers. Four years later it had so developed that there were forty caravans and nearly a hundred workers.

It was indeed the

most splendid training for personal and evangelistic work on the mission field. We were sent out two by two in different districts of the country, and those who had not got a caravan either rented or were offered free a room in one of the cottages in whichever village they made their headquarters. Members of the Band were frequently invited to hold missions in chapels or mission halls which looked as though they would have to be closed, because the congregations had dwindled to almost nothing.

In places where we had not been invited, we first called at the vicarage, if there was one, so that we could explain to the vicar the purpose of our arrival in the village, and express the hope that he would have no objection to our visiting all the houses in order to invite the people to the meetings. Objections, however, were not often made, and we generally received much kindness.

We then started with open air meetings in the village street, not very easy when there were only two people to hold them, as was quite often the case. One sat at the portable harmonium (that was nearly always my job) while the other sang the hymns, and we took it in turns to preach at the empty street and closed doors, but frequently open windows. Then, of course a number of children would collect, and we taught them choruses and invited them to children's meetings in the chapel, church room or mission hall, as the case might be. After a week or two there would generally be a nice little group of people gathered together ready to support us.

There is something infectious and attractive about young and enthusiastic people who apparently are quite willing to make fools of themselves because they are so in earnest, and some of my very happiest memories are of the groups of village youths and girls who would stand rather sheepishly with us at the open air meetings, and later even say a word of testimony themselves, and then crowd into the caravan for hot cocoa and buns and more chorus singing. I can't help laughing as I write all this, and you, too, are probably smiling as you read it. What a Band of red-hot, fervent, ridiculous young people we were! And how we did enjoy it.

I understood exactly what the Lord meant when He said, "You can't put new wine into old bottles, or it will burst the bottles and spill out." The radiant new life which filled me and so many of the other Band workers simply couldn't be cooped up in the old orthodox forms and channels, nor be confined to Sunday services. We were so full of it we simply had to rush out into the streets and highways and by-ways, and among the fields and hedges, and proclaim it to all. I have no doubt we did embarrass and irritate some people, and we certainly often felt fools ourselves, but it was lovely to be a fool for Christ's sake, and we were filled with a radiant joy whenever others were persuaded to follow Him too. I know the wonder of it used to break over me in waves of thankfulness and love to the Lord Jesus.

I could hardly believe that I was the same miserable, morbid person who had longed to commit suicide and escape from the world altogether. And it was the Lord Jesus who had made all the difference and worked the amazing transformation. Then everybody must hear about Him.

One occasion, for some reason or other, often comes back to my memory and stands out with peculiar vividness, I think because it so pointed the contrast between life without Him and life with Him. We were living, at the time, in a tiny self-righteous village, where, nevertheless, all religious life seemed to have died out. The chapel had been closed, and there was no church.

One day I went out visiting alone, while my fellow worker was busy elsewhere, and came to a miserable cottage where, I had been told, a fallen women was living with the third or fourth man for whom she had kept house. When she came to the door in answer to my knock, I saw that she was still almost a girl, just about my own age, thin, sad and slatternly. I said to her something like this, "Please excuse me, but I have come to tell you about the Lord Jesus and the wonderful way He can help you." She stood looking at me while I began to pour it all out, crudely and badly, in my inexperienced way, but she hardly seemed to listen to what I said.

Then suddenly she interrupted in the middle of a sentence. "You are a good girl, aren't you?" she said. "I can see it in your face. You don't know what it is to be bad. Oh I wish I were good too." She burst into tears, ran back into the cottage and shut the door, and I stood out there in the weed-covered garden and thought, with astonished sorrow, "Why am I not in her place and she in mine? Why has God's grace so delivered and transformed me, and she and so many multitudes of others don't know anything about it?"

But the thing which really made life so radiant in those days, and set its lasting impress on me, was the Quaker emphasis laid on the hearing heart, and the close, beautiful fellowship which generally developed between each pair of workers. It was during those four years that I came to realise the absolute necessity of praying with one's fellow worker over every detail, not only of our evangelistic and mission work but also of our own personal relationship, if we were to be able to work together in harmony and preach with conviction.

A caravan is a very small, confined place, and we generally changed partners every few months, so that we had to learn to live and work together with many different members of the Band, whether we were temperamentally suited or not. After our simple caravan housekeeping was finished a good part of every morning was spent in prayer together. We always began with the Quaker habit of sitting in complete silence in His presence, lifting our hearts to Him and asking Him to cleanse our thoughts and show us if there was anything to confess or put right before we began to pray together. We sat there in the quietness, just seeking to realise His presence. Then we began to pray together, simply and informally, as though we were holding conversation with the Lord.

Not only did

we ask Him for His plans for the day but as we were a faith mission and wholly dependent upon Him for all our supplies, we took them from Him in faith. We did not kneel down but sat in His presence talking to Him as we would have done if we had been among His disciples when He was a man in Palestine. We offered ourselves to Him daily, asking Him to use all our faculties, so that we could be made sure of His will and understand His plans for us.

How much I owe to those fellow workers of twenty years ago. When I go home on furlough and meet some of them again, it seems natural to continue fellowship as though it had never been interrupted.

It was my first senior worker who initiated me into the Band ways and taught me the joy and power of praying with another about every detail. When you do that regularly with other people, however different you may be temperamentally or in outlook and background, you cannot help loving the people you pray with and being able to adapt yourself to their different ways. You learn, too, that where two or three are gathered together in that way, the joy and power is doubled or trebled.

There was a great deal for my senior worker to teach me and I did not at all realise my abysmal ignorance. I am sorry to say that, ready and eager as I was to learn all that I could in the realm of spiritual experience, I remained extremely uninterested in the practical, humdrum drudgery of daily life. It seemed to me that, however hard I tried, I never would learn to cook anything eatable, and that in the circumstances it was more sensible and convenient to allow my companion to do that, while I undertook to do the water-carrying, the chimney-cleaning, and to run the errands.

In most cases my partners very patiently and obligingly acquiesced in this scheme, but the time came when one of them firmly declared that I must do my share of cooking and that we would take it in turns on alternate days. She took no notice of my disgust, nor of my pathetic pleadings to be let off on the ground of some inherent incapacity over which I had no control, and the new régime was started. Thereafter she became a martyr to dyspepsia, bitterly complaining that on the days I cooked she could scarcely eat anything, and on the days when she cooked it was the same, as she was still suffering from the effects of the day before.

This unhappy state of affairs was terminated by putting me to work with a partner who also was a hopeless cook and just as uninterested in household things as I was. However, she and I were extremely happy together and as we were on excellent terms with the people of the village where we were working we were either asked out to meals, or some kind friend baked for us. To my shame, it must be confessed that I left the Band almost as inefficient in household management as I entered it, and had to learn in a much harder school later on.

In those days mundane matters appeared to me supremely unimportant—the spiritual was everything. Indeed it seemed almost wrong to spend much time on temporal things, and much more sensible to expect people to ask us out to meals and offer to do our laundry for us. Were we not bringing them unspeakable spiritual blessings, so why should not they look after our temporal needs? How I bless those gracious fellow workers of long ago, who so patiently and generously bore with my irritating selfishness and devastating incapacity. It was a long time before my heart learnt to hear my Lord's voice telling me His will about such mundane things as washing up, dusting, and trying to be tidy. But how patiently He bore with me, and with what faithful friends and fellow workers He has always put me.

However, there was so much else to learn in the Band that did interest me. I had learnt nothing up till then about depending on the Lord for all supplies, and now I had to learn this new kind of dependence too. I will only mention one or two examples of how the Lord instructed us in this lesson, though a whole book could be filled with illustrations. I do not think anyone could work in the Band and continue to suppose that it was presumptuous or irreverent to go to the Lord about the smallest details of daily life, as well as with more important problems. We were dependent upon Him for everything, including the food we ate, and often we did not know how the next meal would be supplied. I will mention almost the first instance which occurred in this matter of His wonderful supply of all our needs, because it played such an important part in my training.

The first place I was sent to after joining the Band was a little scattered village named Angel Bank, up on the Clee Hills in Shropshire. There was a tiny chapel there, belonging to the Ludlow Methodist Circuit, but the attendance at the chapel had dropped to three or four people, and it had been decided to hold a mission in order to try and stir up new spiritual life in the village.

We were the missioners invited. At least my senior worker was. She had worked in the Salvation Army for several years before joining the Society of Friends, and she mixed salvationism and Quakerism together in a way I would never have believed possible, but with astonishingly fruitful results.

One of the local preachers and his wife offered us hospitality in their tiny two-roomed cottage, which stood all alone, far from the main road, and in order to reach it we had either to climb three stiles or open three barred gates. The one bedroom, which they generously gave up to our use, was reached by a step-ladder through a trap-door in the roof of the kitchen. How kind and hospitable they were! There was one precious cow which provided them with delicious milk, butter and cream. But soon after our arrival this cow became very ill and had to be treated with medicine and hot drinks every few hours.

It was a bitterly cold autumn that year and there was a very long-drawn-out coal strike. The little store of coal in the cottage yard dwindled rapidly and could not be replaced, and our kind hosts looked more and more anxious. One particularly cold morning, when the Clee Hills were covered with ice and hoar-frost, I climbed down through the trap-door and found our hostess in tears. "Oh, Miss Hurnard," she said, "I don't know what we are to do, the last little pieces of coal and coal-dust are on the fire now, and we can get no more wood. I have boiled a kettle to make a pot of tea for our breakfast, but there is nothing left with which to cook our dinner, and the cow will not be able to have her treatment and will surely die. My husband was in Ludlow several days ago trying to order coal, but because of this strike there is none to be had, and there won't be any for nobody knows how long."

I must confess I was apalled. I had never been in such circumstances before and had never been obliged to rough it in any way. When we had eaten our frugal breakfast and drunk our last cups of hot tea, with no prospects of a warm meal later on in the day, we climbed back into the little loft for our morning prayertime. My heart was sinking but my senior on the other hand was perfectly buoyant and assured. "O Heavenly Father," she prayed, "Thou knowest the real need there is for more coal. Don't let these kind friends suffer as a result of their hospitality to us, and through using up their little store of coal on our account. Don't let their cow die. Please send them some coal at once."

I said a fervent amen to this prayer, to try to make up for the utter unbelief in my own heart. Of course, one had read of such things in small tracts, but they could hardly happen in real life; certainly not under our present circumstances. We had wrapped ourselves as warmly as possible in our blankets while we prayed, but I was quite stiff with cold as I descended the step-ladder an hour or two later. A tiny flame still flickered in the kitchen grate. Suddenly a voice was heard crying excitedly, "Oh, come quickly, look, there is a coal cart arriving." Unable to believe that I heard aright, I hurried outside, and there, sure enough, a man had just opened the third barred gate, and a coal cart bumped across the last field and emptied a good store of coal into the yard. Hastily the fire was made up, the sick cow got its special treatment (and soon recovered), and we all sat down to a comforting hot meal.

The man told us that a few truck-loads of coal had reached Ludlow the day before, and our local preacher's order was high on the list, and so it came about that, "Before they call I will answer, and while they are yet speaking I will hear." It is not, of course, that prayer changes God, or awakens in Him purposes of love and compassion which He has not already felt. No, it changes us, and therein lies its glory and its purpose. It helps us to utter dependence upon God and gives Him the opportunity to confirm our trust in Him and experience His grace in a way which would be absolutely impossible otherwise. He has got everything ready and planned in order to meet all our needs before ever we realise what they are.

But in order to teach us this joy of utter dependence and trust, He waits for us to ask. And perhaps He allows us to miss a very great deal and suffer needless deprivations just because we say, "Prayer doesn't change God and He knows what I need." No, prayer doesn't change God, but not to make our requests known in joyful trust does deprive Him of the joy of granting our requests, and it does deprive us of the joy of experiencing His loving, intimate interest in every detail of our lives. It was the Lord Jesus Himself who said, "Ye have not because ye ask not. Ask and ye shall receive."

A year or two later I was caravanning in the "wild West" of Ireland, in County Sligo, where Roman Catholicism was very strong and Protestants most unpopular. There were bullet-holes in the van we had just taken over from two young men evangelists, as the van had been fired on by fanatics and the young men had been obliged to escape, leaving their dinner half cooked in the saucepan. It was thought that women evangelists would not be molested in the same way, and so it proved—although there was plenty of other opposition.

The only place we could get, in which to hold our meetings, was an empty chicken house. This we cleaned out, disinfected and adorned with flowers, and placed in it a table, two rows of chairs and the portable harmonium. for the first few nights scarcely anybody came inside the chicken house, but quite a crowd gathered outside, throwing stones which rattled on the corrugated iron roof in a deafening cascade. Later, when the people's confidence had been won, the chicken house was crowded out night after night and proved too small, and the missioners had to take attaché-cases with them to every service in which groceries, which the people, with true Irish hospitality, lavished upon them.

But before that happened there were some weeks of real difficulty, and I remember one week-end when there was nothing in the van for dinner or supper except bread and tea. Of course it would have done us no harm in the world to live for a day or two on bread and water, but somehow it was not what we expected a rich Heavenly Father to permit when we were out on His business. And while we were at morning prayer in the caravan we prayed simply and earnestly, "Dear Heavenly Father, please send us something else." We were still at prayer when there was a knock on the door, and on opening it we found the postman, who handed in a large square parcel which had just arrived from Dublin, the other side of the country. On opening it we found a plump roast fowl, wrapped in fresh, still-crisp cabbage leaves.

A whole book, as I have already said, could be filled with stories of the same kind and of answered prayer in many, many matters quite apart from the supply of our temporal needs. We were constantly having it brought home to us in wonderful ways that God always has enough ready and waiting to meet our needs, no matter what they may be, and no matter how impossible the circumstances look.

I do believe that in the early years of Christian experience He often meets our needs in striking ways in order to strengthen and confirm our new and weak faith, and perhaps He does not leave us to wait long for the answers to our prayers for the same reason. But the more experience of His goodness and faithfulness we have, and the longer we have proved Him, the more He is able to test and develop our faith by teaching us long-suffering and the assurance to wait patiently even if the answer tarries. But whenever we say truly from the heart, "I am ready" for God's will whatever it is, we shall certainly experience His faithfulness and providential dealings in ways which to other people will often appear extraordinary.

Quite often one hears people saying, "Nothing spectacular in the way of answered prayer ever happens to me." But perhaps something a little more spectacular in the way of faith is required first, for after all faith is being willing to test the faithfulness of God, and one cannot often do that secretly and safely. It generally means openly taking some sort of risk and of being willing to look a fool before others.

If somebody says, "I never feel sure enough as to what God's will is to be able to take such a risk," may not that be just the point? You would be made sure if you were willing to take the risk of being allowed to look a fool. I think very few true disciples of the Lord Jesus are allowed always to appear sensible and correct. We all have to appear as fools in the eyes of the world at some time or other. For, after all, pride is the greatest cause of unbelief and unreality in spiritual things, and looking foolish is one of the ways by which we take up the cross and crucify our pride. And it is not likely that the Lord of Love will let us by-pass the way of weakness and foolishness altogether.

Often people who are naturally gifted with a lot of common sense and organising ability find it very difficult to believe that any guidance can be right which looks foolish or contrary to common sense, and are never willing to accept such guidance. In that case it is difficult for them to develop the hearing heart, and they go through life largely dependent on their own judgment.

On the other hand impulsive people go to the other extreme, and often find it difficult to distinguish between their own sudden, strong impulses to act in a certain way, and the promptings of the Holy Spirit. Of course impulses and a tremdous urge can come from the enemy as well as from our Lord, and if we are inclined to act impulsively and impetuously, it is essential to check up each time and honestly consider the results that follow afterwards. If the impulse often proves to have been fruitless, a mistake, or impossible to put into execution, then there is clear indication that one needs to go very humbly to the Lord as a little child, and talk to Him about this tendency to mistake impulses for guidance and to be enabled to learn the lesson of yielding all our thought processes to Him that He may check and direct our thoughts.

It will mean real discipline, too, in our thinking (no indulging in delightful daydreams about ourselves), care over the books we read, and the way we employ our thoughts in our free time. Often, at first, it will demand open, sincere confession to others that we were mistaken, and a humble, unresentful acceptance of their reminder that we often are!

I am sure, in those early years in the Band, we young workers often made mistakes and followed our own thoughts rather than God's plans. And then, of course, there was failure, but we knew that we had to admit it honestly and openly and say "we hurried before Him and it has proved wrong." However, in all these twenty-six years I joyfully confess that I have never known the Lord to let me down or allow me to make a mistake when I was honestly longing to do His will.

There have been many times when the things I thought He was telling me to do looked absolutely crazy and I have said, "Lord, I must be imagining this or going queer in my head." But He has never once, as far as I can judge, allowed me to make a mistake if I was really willing to obey. Sometimes He has intervened to prevent the mistake being made just as He promises in His Words, "Thine ears shall hear a word behind thee saying, This is the way, walk ye in it, when ye turn to the right or to the left." Far more often it has turned out in after-experience that the crazy-looking thing was actually the right thing, and the one essential action for that particular time.

There have also been other times when I quite misunderstood the ultimate purpose for which He was preparing me by some strange-looking act of obedience, but every time I have acted in obedience to what I believed to be His will it has always turned out to be the perfect preparation for the real purpose He Himself had in mind. For He does often cause us to walk in darkness, having no light at all on the extraordinary path by which He is leading us, but then His precious assurance is, "What I do thou knowest not now, but thou shalt know hereafter."

One other lesson I also learnt, while I was in the Band, which has meant a great deal to me since. I was staying with an old Quaker lady while I was conducting some meetings in the North of England, and one day she said to me, "My dear, it is nice to see a young person so full of joy in serving the Lord as thou art. Let me say something to thee. If ever the time comes when thee is tempted to serve Him grudgingly, or to shrink from the cost, or to begin to talk of making sacrifices for Him, will thee remember this: 'Sacrifice is the ecstasy of giving the best we have to the One we love the most.'"

There have been times since then when I have been tempted to think He asked too much, more than I could give, when for a few moments submission or obedience have looked too costly to be possible. Only for a moment or two, thank God, for during those moments I have had an appalling glimpse into that awful existence where He is not known and not obeyed, which is hell. Then He has gently brought me back to this glorious truth: that sacrifice is indeed the ecstasy of giving the best we have to the One we love the most. When that is the experience of the heart, sorrow and disappointment and heartache become sweeter than the greatest natural happiness.

4

LAUNCH OUT INTO THE DEEP

Christ the Lord hath sent me
  Through the midnight lands,
Mine the ordination
  Of the nail-pierced hands.

After I had been working in the Evangelistic Band for four years I was sent over to Ireland again to do deputation work, travelling over the country telling about the needs of the unevangelised villages of England and Ireland. One Saturday afternoon I was invited to go with a party of factory and shop girls on an outing to Ireland's Eye, one of the beauty spots near Dublin. After a time I wandered away alone and climbed to the highest rocky peak. It was indescribably lovely, the tiny island surrounded by blue sea and spanned by the blue sky, and seagulls with dazzlingly white wings wheeling around in their multitudes. I felt a great awe and joy fill my heart, and my whole being cried out to the Creator of that beauty that I might be helped to worship and adore, and to hear His voice.

When I went out that morning I had no idea that God

was going to speak to me in a special way, or that I was to receive a clear call which once again would revolutionise my whole way of life. I still felt that eventually the Lord wanted me to become a missionary, but I had no idea where that would be, and I was extraordinarily happy in the Band and could not help hoping that I would be allowed to work there for some time to come. But up there on that rocky throne, lifted between the earth and the sky, I began to feel a deep inner certainty that God had brought me there for a purpose, and was going to speak about something special.

I remembered Abraham and that wherever he travelled and God met him he built an altar. I too longed to build another altar, to offer myself wholly again to the Lord, ready for whatever He might be wanting me to do. As far as I could understand up there on the rocks, there was no particularly difficult task ahead and no known act of costly obedience, so I simply built the altar, as it were, by offering my whole being again to the Lord and lifting up to Him my will, just as I did daily, but now with a sense that there was some special, new significance in it. Then I turned to His loved Word, still His love-letters to me, and even more precious than four years before.

Up there on Ireland's Eye, I had no special subject in mind, and began to read just where the Bible opened, which happened to be the ninth chapter of Daniel. I saw at once that it described how Daniel went apart to pray to the Lord, and it seemed to fit in with my own thoughts at the time, and I read on, pondering and meditating upon Daniel, the "man greatly beloved" by his God. As I read how he went apart to fast and pray for his people Israel, I was struck by the amazing way in which he completely identified himself with his nation in their sin and their rebellion against God, for which they had been carried into captivity.

And yet Daniel himself had not sinned with them in this way, far from it. From the first he had kept himself unspotted from idolatry, even after having been carried away captive to one of the most wicked and idolatrous courts in the world. Yet here he was, praying as one completely identified with them in their sin and need of God's pardon and restoration. "I prayed unto the Lord and made my confession and said, O Lord we have sinned and committed iniquity and done wickedly and rebelled . . . neither have we harkened unto Thy servants the prophets . . . O Lord, righteousness belongeth unto Thee, but unto us confusion of face . . . O Lord hear . . O Lord forgive . . . O Lord hearken and do."

As I slowly read through this wonderful prayer, pondering on it verse by verse and marvelling at the passion of humility and longing love which made this wonderful and holy man able to identify himself so completely with his rebellious and backsliding people the Jews, an unexpected and startling thing happened. A thought came into my mind, as though naturally following the train of previous thoughts, but with a clarity and significance which seemed a personal challenge.

"Hannah, would you be willing to identify yourself with the Jewish people in the same way, if I asked you to?"

I sat amazed and thought about it. The year before, in 1929, my father had taken my brother and myself for a two months' tour through the Holy Land, beginning at Aleppo in the north of Syria, and finishing in Palestine. He was deeply interested in all the Armenian refugee camps then still existing in Syria, and wished to see something of the new Jewish settlements in Palestine, which he looked upon as a wonderful fulfilment of prophecy.

My brother and I were delighted beyond measure to visit so many places mentioned in the Bible, especially to see the hills of Galilee and walk beside the lake which the Lord Jesus had so loved. But we were both bored stiff at having to visit modern Jewish agricultural settlements, and whenever possible we left father to visit such places with a guide and made off on our own, either for the open country or for the seashore.

We both agreed that we found modern Zionism unattractive, and I myself felt an inner antipathy for the Jewish people I met, the reason for which I could not have defined, even to myself, merely deciding, "I don't care for them and I'm glad I don't have to live among them." Now as I sat there on Ireland's Eye, and tried in memory to recall the Jewish people and their settlements in Palestine and, as I considered it, their dreary new town of Tel-Aviv, built on the sand, the thought came again, "Hannah, are you willing to go to Palestine and live and work among the Jews, and identify yourself with them completely?" And I found my thoughts answering Him in great distress.

"But, Lord, I'm sorry to say I don't like the Jews a bit. They are the last people in the world I feel interested in trying to help. How could I be of any use as a missionary to the Jews if I don't like them?"

"If you will yield to Me wholly and agree to go, I will make you able to love them and identify yourself with them. It all depends upon your will."

At a time like that, when the reality of the Lord's presence was so real that it seemed as though only a thin veil hid Him from sight, I often found myself speaking aloud as though holding a conversation with a visible companion. And now I scrambled to my feet and knelt down on the rock which had become an altar, for this was a definite offering of myself, an act of deep worship and glad surrender. It concluded a conversation and sealed my readiness to obey. I knelt then on the rocks and said, "Here I am, Lord. I will go as a missionary to Thy people Israel." As simple and unprepared and unexpected as that. Immediately the "yes" was said my heart glowed with an awed and amazed joy. "Oh, how privileged I am to be called and sent to work in the very land where my Lord lived and worked Himself, and to become identified with the people of Israel.

But when I came down from the rocky peak of Ireland's Eye, and began to tell my friends that God had called me to go to Palestine as a missionary, how little, how absurdly little, there was to show for it. The friend with whom I was staying asked how I knew I had a call and how it came to me. I could only say vaguely, through reading Daniel 9, and she looked dubious and felt that one would need a more definite and practical sign that God meant one to take such a tremendous step. Is it ever possible to make another really understand what one hears with the heart and not with the ears?

When I told the leader of the Band I felt that God was now calling me to the mission field, namely, to Palestine, he and others with him were at first very doubtful. They told me that my place clearly seemed to be in the Band. God was blessing and using the witness there, and there was as wide a field for service in the villages of our own land as on the mission field, and I was probably not strong enough to work abroad in a hot country.

It was harder still when, after more prayer for guidance, I wrote to the secretary of the only interdenominational mission that I knew which was working in Palestine, and offered my services. Among the questions sent to me to answer was, naturally enough, one about special training and qualifications, and another asking why I felt called to Jewish work in Palestine, and there was nothing that I could explain except a "still small voice" speaking through my thoughts at Ireland's Eye, saying "Will you go and identify yourself with My people Israel?"

I answered the questions to the best of my ability and in due course a letter came back saying they had noted that I had no special qualifications, as a trained nurse or teacher or secretary, all of which they were needing, but there was, at present, no opening for a lady evangelist. Among the Jews, I was told, women were not generally considered worth listening to if they tried to preach to or teach men. But in a few months' time the mission doctor from Haifa would be coming to England on furlough, and then, if I still felt sure of God's call, I could apply again.

When the doctor came, I went to see him. He was a wisely cautious man, and determined that I should be under no illusions about working in the Holy Land. He said that the climate of Haifa was hot and damp, and not suitable for highly strung temperaments, and that nervous "break-downs" were common. He also emphasised that they did not want anyone to join them temporarily for short-time service, but only people who would look upon it as their real life-work. "Are you willing to leave your bones in Palestine, if necessary, Miss Hurnard?" he enquired, and I replied that if the Lord's return tarried I believed I was.

He then persisted, "What makes you suppose that God is calling you to work among Jews in Palestine? Why not Jews in London, or in Europe, or perhaps in Egypt? Have you thought, for instance, of offering to help in the school for Jews in Cairo?" I replied meekly that I had not, as I had never trained as a teacher, and I thought the Lord had said Palestine.

"Look here," he said, "we do need a

fully trained nurse and also a secretary, but not at present an untrained gap filler, and it is very important not to make a mistake. Will you go home and ask the Lord about it all over again, just as though you had never received a call? See if the Lord confirms it, or if He is trying to make you understand that He wants you to work among Jews in London or Egypt. There is such a glamour about the Holy Land. All sorts of queer people come out believing themselves called to a special work in Jerusalem, or on a crusade to the dear Jews. You go and see if God doesn't say, I want you in London or Cairo, and then let me know."

So I went home determined to do as the doctor suggested, but more than ever puzzeled and concerned that I had nothing of definite practical significance with which to convince those concerned that God had called me. I went to my room and said, "Oh, please Lord Jesus, do teach me and guide me. Make me sure of Thy will. Was I only imagining it all at Ireland's Eye? Do you really prefer me to work in London or Cairo?"

I opened by Bible meaning to read until I came to some comforting word of assurance that the Lord would not let me make a mistake. But, as it happened, the very first words my eyes fell on were God's call to Moses, "Come now and I will send thee to . . . Egypt" (Exodus 3:10).

I could not help laughing. "Lord," I exclaimed, "if You meant me to go to the school for Jewish children in Cairo, why didn't You lead me to train as a teacher? And why did You say

Palestine at Ireland's Eye?"

Again in my thoughts I had that curious rest and assurance which He gives us when we have understood His will, and none of the uneasy uncertainty and questioning which generally means we have not yet heard all that He wants to say on a matter, probably because we are not willing to hear it.

And once again I realised that here was another clear illustration of the principle that guidance cannot safely be received through verses on a page of the Bible opened at random (though such chance openings do often supply us with words of comfort and strength in our times of need), but can only be accepted as guidance when the Lord plainly confirms to us in other ways, and clearly indicates by further signs following, that this chance lighting on a verse of Scripture really was a part of His will for us and is the guidance we were seeking.

One great encouragement I had during that time of testing was the delighted joy of my father when I told him that I believed that God was calling me to work among the Jews in Palestine. "Thy mother and I dedicated thee to the Lord before thou wast born," he said, "and we always hoped that the Lord would call thee, if it were His will, to work among the Jews." Many years later he wrote to me in a treasured letter that the fact that he had a daughter privileged to work among God's people Israel, in their ancient homeland, had been the greatest joy and satisfaction that he had known in life.

It seemed

wonderful and beautiful, as I thought about it, that there on Ireland's Eye, in that quiet, still, small voice, the Lord had been able to make me sure of His will, and in responding to that will to be the answer to the secret, earnest prayers my parents had prayed ever since my birth. They had indeed told me that they had dedicated me to the Lord, but they had never hinted that they had prayed and hoped that I might be called as a missionary to the Jews.

My mother had died, when I was twenty years old, while I was still in my first year of training at Ridgelands. I had been called home from the training school just a few days before she died. It had been an immense joy to her, during the last year of her life when she suffered a great deal and had had to give up nearly all her speaking and preaching engagements, that she could say when she had to refuse requests to speak at meetings, "But my daughter will take my place."

Oh, how thankful I had been that the Lord allowed the great change to take place in me a year before she died, and that she had this joy of seeing her unhappy, difficult and morbid daughter, who had never shown any affection or love, thus transformed and made willing to help in the work she loved best. When I came home a few days before she died she was in terrible pain and sometimes wandering, but in one of the lucid intervals just before she died, I was standing by her bedside, and my grandmother who was sitting there said, "Hannah, promise your mother that you will stay at home with your father and look after him when mother herself can no longer do it. You are the special daughter for this. Promise her now."

My heart nearly stood still. I had been converted only one year, and had promised the Lord to go abroad as a missionary. And here I was being challenged at my mother's death-bed to give it all up, though I knew that mother herself had delighted in the thought of my going. Had she changed now and did she think it more important that I should stay at home?

"Promise, Hannah," repeated my grandmother. "You must set her mind at rest." Then I looked at my mother in her pain and utter weakness, and cried out to her for help. "Mother, do you really want me to make this promise?"

She opened her eyes painfully, almost too weary and exhausted to speak, and said faintly, using the old Quaker speech which she and our father still used to their children, "I thought thee felt the Lord was calling thee to be a missionary?"

"I do, I do," I cried earnestly. "You know I am training for it. I do think He has called me."

"Then don't ever allow anything to hinder thee going," she said. "Do His will whatever happens. Father wants that too."

Those were the last clear words she ever spoke to me. So my mother, just as my father had done as Keswick, fully and with all her heart gave me to be a missionary. How can I ever bless the Lord sufficiently for such parents as mine? How can I ever express the debt I owe them?

But every step of the way out to the mission field was tested. The doctor, as well as most of my friends, did not think that my health or nervous temperament fitted me to work abroad, and I could not but agree with them. Indeed I considered that aspect of the matter with great apprehension and the enemy made a great "scarecrow" out of it. But I felt that it must be just another opportunity for turning my fear of breaking down into faith.

Beside that, I knew that as I had no practical training I could not expect a missionary society to employ me as a salaried missionary if they were not needing an evangelistic worker. But in the end it was agreed that I should go to Haifa on trial, paying my own expenses and undertaking to assist in any way in which I proved capable, being ready to act as a "stop-gap" wherever required, until it could be seen what work the Lord really wanted me to do, or would open for me. Oh, how deeply thankful I was to the mission, and how thankful I have remained ever since, for the loving, patient way they accepted me during those first difficult years abroad when I could do so little for them.

In the end I crept meekly, and oh so thankfully, into Palestine on January 21st, 1932. And what a stripping and breaking process then began.

5

HOW BEAUTIFUL UPON THE MOUNTAINS

Lord Crucified, give me a heart like Thine,
Teach me to love the dying souls of men,
And keep my heart in closest touch with Thee
And give me Love, pure Calvary Love
To win the lost for Thee.

If it difficult to keep the daily quiet time, and to maintain close, intimate fellowship with the Lord Jesus in a Christian country, one finds it infinitely more so on the mission field, among multitudes who do not know Him and are often definitely antagonistic to Him. Such daily, unbroken communion, however, is the one vital necessity upon which everything depends, and without which, however warm the desire to help and serve may be, the missionary will prove powerless to bring any souls into vital, transforming contact with the Lord Jesus.

The enemy of souls, of course, knows this and does his utmost to hinder the keeping of the daily quiet time. Almost anything will prove easier than to form this daily habit, for so many factors combine to prevent it. First there is the strangeness of everything, the complete uprooting of all the old ties and habits and customs, leaving one feeling unsettled, restless, tired, and with the continual sense of being in a strange environment to which one only slowly and painfully becomes adjusted.

Then there are the endless irrations and nerve-racking difficulties due to lack of the new language and the misunderstandings arising from this ignorance. Also the difficulty of adjusting oneself to the completely different outlook of those among whom one has gone to work. Then perhaps there are the primitive conditions and lack of conveniences to which one has been accustomed; and above all, the change of climate.

For the first four years, in the hot, damp, enervating climate of Haifa, I never felt really well or ready to face a new day's work. I was happy, and joyously thankful to be there, but night after night as I dragged myself to bed, I was so weary and aching from head to foot I often found myself crying as I undressed. Then to rise early each morning for my quiet time (often at four o'clock) really seemed impossibly difficult, especially as I generally lay tossing wearily through the long hot nights and only slept towards morning.

Everyone goes through their own individual testings and strains and struggles of one sort or another during their first years abroad, and that which I personally found hardest was battling with physical weariness and the exhaustion of trying to do work to which I was unaccustomed, though it was made as easy and light as possible for me. Then, after the happy years of preaching up and down the country, to find myself completely cut off, through lack of language, from all the old activities, was painfully frustrating.

Now, too, I was a member of a mission, the other members of which were all devoted and spiritually-minded Christians, who worked to a time-table and had their own and differing duties. Gone was the close, intimate, ceaseless fellowship in prayer about every detail of the work to which I had been accustomed with all my fellow workers in the Band. Now there was one weekly staff prayer meeting during which each one prayed in turn, or perhaps not at all, and the old Presbyterian minister who led this meeting did not greatly approve of warm, spontaneous outpourings which savoured to him of over-familiarity with the Lord; and I found these new staff prayer meetings painfully chilling and repressive.

I could see at once, and daily came to prove it, that in all practical Christian living, and loving service and true self-forgetfulness, these new fellow workers were all miles in advance of anything I had yet attained. Their lives and service shamed me to the heart. But oh how I did long for someone to pray with! This however was rather discouraged as likely to lead to cliquishness and perhaps to a rather self-righteous attitude of praying that others might become a little more spiritually-minded. This was an entirely new point of view to me, and as time passed I came to see there was sound wisdom in it.

Then, too, the

Sunday services were so unlike those to which I had been accustomed. They were conducted morning and evening by the old minister, who often prefaced his sermons with the remark, "I first preached this address in the year 1888 or 1890," and he used this collection of sermons again and again. They were both learned and truly instructive, but it was a great shock to me, for I had been trained to think that no "stale" spiritual food should be offered but only that which came warm and new from the heart.

I have since come to realise that even zealous evangelical preachers of the gospel are liable to the same danger of falling into stereotyped repetition, without perhaps the same honesty in confessing it. But in those early days it seemed to me that of fresh, vital spiritual food there was none, and never before had I so needed to be empowered and strengthened to meet the battles and struggles of everyday life.

In actual fact this was all part of the new discipline and development which the Lord saw I must now undergo. It was exactly what was needed next. For bubbling, frothing new wine cannot continue to spill and splash over for ever. It must be constrained and confined in some way, or it will never become mellowed and sweetened and made ready for its best use.

And in spite of what seemed such difficult repression, those were happy years, not, indeed, with the irrepressible joy and lightheartedness of the former years but with a growing sense of the Lord' gentle disciplining and of deepening union with Him. For, cut off from all the warm inspiring services I had been accustomed to, with no one to pray with day by day, and what seemed so few opportunities to witness, the early morning quiet times became more and more important and blessed. An hour was never enough, two or more became the daily allotment. And during those precious, hard-won periods, I was forced to thrust deeper and deeper into the river of His love and grace, for the sources of my spiritual life no longer lay near the surface.

Looking back on these nineteen years, my life seems to have taken its whole significance and pattern from those early quiet times and what I remember most clearly is a succession of radiant morning hours in the secret of His presence, listening to Him and then going out to try and put into practice the things He said. The daily happenings in between those golden hours seem far less significant, though, after the first four years, the days themselves were often adventurous and exciting enough, one would have thought, to make a lasting impression on the memory.

But the outward happenings and adventures on such a mission field as seething, restless, riot-disturbed Palestine, seem to pale into dimness in comparison with the tremendous significance of those hours alone with Him. The visible life was tossed and strained and disturbed by events on the surface, but as C. S. Lewis says, I have "never lived anywhere but in heaven." For the roots of that life were in the soil of heaven itself, the reality of God's presence. And who that has not experienced it can even begin to understand the joy, the security, the blessed sense of the immense worthwhileness of life, developed by living in the invisible world where all things are eternal.

The days and months passed, full of work in the medical clinic, taking English classes in the evening and studying the language, and so my first four years on the mission field came to an end.

Then the secret, still small voice spoke again, simply and quietly, during one of those staff prayer meetings which I have already mentioned. The Lord told me that now I was to begin doing in Palestine just what I had done in England. I was to visit every Jewish settlement in the neighbourhood, going from house to house, knocking on every door and offering God's Word to everyone I met, trying to speak to every person thus contacted, about the Lord Jesus Christ.

It looked utterly mad to try to do in a non-Christian land, where most people were hostile and antagonistic to the Lord Jesus, the same kind of work, which even in Christian England had never been simple or easy. Why, many of those people to whom I believed He was now calling me to go were bound by their religious principles to spit whenever I mentioned the name of my Lord and to say, "May the name and the memory of that blasphemer be blotted out."

Moreover, this new call came in 1936, just at the time when the Arab riots against the Jews, which were to last three years, broke out in their fury. During that time the roads in the country were infested with mines, buses and cars were the targets for snipers, and for nearly three years no civilian cars were allowed on the roads unless they were in military-protected convoys.

When the call came to start out visiting, in the little Austin car the Lord then gave me, all the settlements in the country, as well as those in the immediate neighbourhood of Haifa, a new emergency rule had just been passed that no civilians could drive their cars on the roads outside the cities without permission from the authorities, and then only for the most important reasons. But there was one curious omission in this new regulation. When I went to the office to ask for a permit to allow me to travel alone on those outlawed roads, I was told the new regulation did not refer to women drivers, so for the next two years my little baby Austin was practically the only civilian car still free to run about all over the country alone.

Of course, I was constantly stopped and questioned by the police and military, who expressed amazement and sometimes consternation that women could still drive about, but the rule was never amended. Indeed there was little reason in one way why it should have been, for the Arab terrorists during those years never molested women. But, of course, road mines and outbreaks of shooting were widespread.

During those years many British friends and missionaries told us that it was wrong and inconsiderate to the British authorities to continue doing such work. It would greatly add to their difficulties if we were attacked or molested and kidnapped. And we made this aspect of the subject a real matter for prayer.

The Lord had given a clear call, and when some of us started to obey that call, He provided us with three cars and all the necessary equipment. But only fanatics will insist on pushing forward without pausing at every step to ask the Lord if they are still to proceed and are still in His will.

I believe this is a very important point in guidance. I find that when the Lord calls to some act of obedience which looks absurd, or doubtful, or even wrong, it is necessary to take the first step in obedience without paying any attention to doubts or fears. But when we have begun to obey, then we must go to the Lord with all our questionings and the criticism of others, to ask if we are still to proceed or if there is anything we should modify or change. Always begin to obey, and after every new step ask if it is His will that we should keep going forward. He is faithful, and will check us if we have not really understood His mind. But it is hopeless to wait for further guidance or confirmation from the Lord until we have begun to obey in faith.

So in this matter of travelling during the riots, we continually sought the Lord's will, and He continually called us to go forward in it. His special promise was "Ye shall go out with joy, and be led forth in peace" (Isa. 55:12). And so it proved. We had friends whose cars were riddled with bullets, and sometimes we came to places where the road had just been blown up, or passed through some area where just afterwards shooting took place, but no harm of any kind ever came to us, and we never had to appeal to the police or military for help or protection.

On more than one occasion during those years, when we were preaching in Moslem villages, there were armed men from these terrorist gangs among those who gathered to listen to us, and who thus had the chance of hearing the gospel message. And although the British authorities at that time were having to put down these armed gangs by force and punish the Arab villages which gave them shelter, and though we often arrived to preach in such villages where the military had been taking punitive measures, British though we were, we were never molested or ill-treated.

Then came the Second World War, and although the riots died down during those years, the visiting was again in grave danger of being stopped. From the very beginning of the war, petrol was drastically rationed, and soon all civilian cars were again ordered off the roads. By that time God had given me three cars, and there was a Band of devoted wholehearted helpers.

Again the seemingly miraculous happened, for we were actually granted extra petrol rations, and not until practically every Jewish settlement and Moslem village in the country had been visited at least once did we have to take the cars off the roads. But even then I was granted a three months' extension by the authorities in order to finish reaching every single place. It is a matter of exceeding thankfulness to us that under the British mandate, as far as we know and according to the latest and most careful survey map which the government brought out, the glorious gospel of the Lord Jesus was preached or Scriptures distributed in every single place in Palestine.

We never knew why, from the human standpoint, this strange chain of favouring circumstances took place. But in 1936 when God gave His call in that little upper room in Haifa where we had gathered for our staff prayer meeting, the promise He gave was, "Behold I have set before thee an open door, and no man can shut it." And it became perfectly obvious that nothing could shut it until every place had been reached and the good tidings made known at least once in every Jewish settlement and Moslem village.

It was in 1938 that God gave me the second part of His call, namely, to take the gospel to every single Arab village in the country as well as to all the Jewish settlements. That really did look crazy, for there were at least three times as many villages as Jewish settlements, and I had never learnt a single word of Arabic, and knew nothing about Moslem work. But God had His chosen messengers scattered all over the land, in many different missions, ready and glad to go out when the way opened.

Some of us became God's chauffeurs and drove His messengers in the three cars He had provided, until by the end of five years (1941) the task was accomplished. Only a few years later came the end of the British mandate and the Arab-Jewish war, when scores and scores, perhaps hundreds, of those same Arab villages became deserted ruins and their inhabitants refugees in neighbouring Moslem countries. Then we understood why God had set the door of opportunity so wide open, and held it open, so that no man was able to shut it. It was His purpose that every place should have the opportunity of hearing the Gospel before the fire of war swept through the land and hundreds of thousands of its inhabitants were scattered.

I have written fully about the adventures and joys of those wonderful years in *Wayfarer in the Land,* and only mention them here because of the wonderful additional proof which they give that He does make His sheep hear His voice. It is safe to trust Him and step out in obedience every time He calls, even though from a human point of view it may look utterly impossible or crazy to try and obey.

Sometimes I think back with an almost overwhelming sense of awe and amazement to that little room near Keswick in 1924 where a stammering, terrified girl knelt by her bedside and cried out desperately, "I can't yield, and He is not real. O God if you are real make Yourself known to me." How could I ever have dreamt at that time of what His love had laid up in store for me.

His purposes will ripen fast,
Unfolding hour by hour,
The bud may have a bitter taste
But sweet will be the flower.

6
ALL THE PROMISES SEEM CONTRADICTED

Lie still and let Him mould thee,
O Lord I would obey;
Thou art the mighty Potter,
And I the yielding clay.
Bend me, Oh bend me to Thy will,
While in Thine hand I'm lying still.

During the war years it was almost impossible to get spare parts for cars, and when every place in Palestine had been reached and all civilian cars were taken off the roads we sold two of the cars which God had given for this evangelistic work, as they were very much the worse for wear and tear. But I myself was allowed to keep and use the third car as I lived right out in the wilds in the little Moslem town of Beisan in the Jordan Valley.

But by 1946, this third car was also terribly decrepit, and repairs cost an almost prohibitive price. Tyres were still unobtainable, and for years it had been unsafe to leave any car standing in the streets, as people came along and jacked up the cars and made off with as many wheels as they had time to remove, and sold them in the black market for £50 or £100 each, according to the condition they were in.

I went to stay in Jerusalem for a few months, after my dear fellow worker, Elizabeth Neatby, was invalided home, but by December of that year I hardly dared venture out in the car, except on the best of high-roads, for I always expected it would break down and leave me stranded.

By this time, however, there was a group of young Arab and Armenian Christians in Jerusalem who had become eager to join in the evangelistic work, and it was my dearest hope and expectation that God would let me train some of these young Palestinian Christians for the itinerant work, so that in a year or two there would be a band of Christians witnessing in every place from end to end of the country. But I was one of the very few missionaries still left in possession of a car, although it was in a shocking condition.

One morning I was driving three special friends to Bethlehem for the monthly prayer day in connection with this evangelistic work. It was always held in Miss Brown's house (C.M.S.) and was one of the highlights of the month to which we all looked forward. For on such prayer days, when we all came together as a group, setting aside the whole day and fixing no time when we must stop, the Lord seemed to be present with us in the most wonderful way, guiding our prayers and revealing His plans and purposes.

On this particular morning as I met my three friends in Jerusalem in order to drive them to Bethlehem, I said to them imploringly, "Please do sit down very gently, the back axle broke the other day, and though it has been patched up it may go again at the least jar. And my spare wheel either fell off or was taken off while we were out visiting last week, so if we have a puncture on the way, we shall just be stranded."

They were all accustomed to these dismal exhortations from me, but that morning as I drove slowly and carefully along the high-road to Bethlehem, one of them suddenly said, "You know I feel the time has come when we really must ask God to give Hannah another car. How can she possibly take out these keen young Christians unless He gives her a strong new car. Let us ask Him this morning to do so."

I was startled and quite taken aback, for although she was only voicing my own constant feeling, it looked so impossible to obtain a car that actually I had never thought of asking the Lord for a new one. So I said hesitatingly, "But think of the tremendous price that cars cost now, more than twice as much as before the war, and I could not afford to buy one. Even if I could afford it, it would be impossible to get one, for the waiting list for new cars is already two years long, and permits are only being granted to priority cases, such as government officials and doctors. I am afraid there is no possibility at all of getting one at this stage."

She, however, was quite undaunted. "Well surely," she said, "it doesn't matter that we can't see how it can be done? You must have a car for the work, and these young Christians are ready and waiting to begin. Surely we have a right to ask our Heavenly Father to give you one. For it must be a priority case in His estimation." And as she spoke it came to all four of us with extraordinary assurance that this was what we were to ask for. We spoke of it at the prayer meeting, and without exception or question the whole group felt the same assurance that we were to ask the Lord for a new car. We did so, and thanked Him in anticipation.

Exactly two weeks after that prayer meeting, I drove the brand-new car home to my garage, and took the whole group out to Bethlehem in it for the next monthly prayer day.

It came to pass in this way. We were given such assurance at the prayer meeting that it was God's will to give a new car for the work, that after driving my three friends to their homes I went straight on to the Morris Car Agency, and asked the manager what prospects there were of being able to buy a new car. He shrugged his shoulders, "None at all, I'm afraid. The priority waiting list is already so long that it will take two years to meet the need. I am afraid ordinary people will have to wait much longer than that before they are granted permits." Then he smiled and added, "But if you care to buy a Morris Eight commercial van, I can let you have one at once. We have two of this year's models still unsold, and it is not necessary to obtain a permit for a commercial van."

I looked at him rather blankly. Was I to drive about in a

margarine or bread van? But he was a practised and gifted salesman and went on persuasively, "You might find a van very convenient for your work, Miss Hurnard. They are built high off the ground and so are particularly practical on hard, rocky tracks. You do not need anything upholstered or chromium plated on such rough journeys as you undertake. And, moreover, they are much cheaper than a saloon car or any other kind of vehicle. It is true they only have two seats, but if you wish, you can have another put in the back. I can show you one of the vans now, if you care to look at it."

Then it came to my heart with the most startling assurance that this was the very thing we needed for our village work. The van would hold all our camping equipment, and it was actually just long enough to sleep in if necessary. It was far more practical for the village work we had in mind than a Morris Minor saloon would have been. There was nothing to spoil. The engine was extremely good, and if we needed to put four or five people in it when we went out preaching in the villages, it would be no real hardship to sit on the floor.

The van cost £460, but I was assured that I could get £200 at least for my old car, decrepit as it was. I went home and prayed about it, and next day sent a wire to my father, and a letter, asking if he were willing for me to buy it, using some money I could realise with his permission. He wired back to say yes, and he and my brother wished to help with it too. So after a few necessary alterations were made in the van, including a third seat, a cupboard for literature and a chest for stores, I sold the old car and, as I mentioned before, drove the new one home in two weeks' time.

That was only the beginning of a most extraordinary train of circumstances, which as I look back on them are so amazing as to seem almost incredible.

That God should have led us all to pray unitedly for a car at that particular time when it was only possible to buy a closed van with no side windows, and what that meant to me and many others later on, perhaps even saving life, and all the ensuing circumstances and adventures in which that van was involved, make a most astonishing story.

At the end of December 1946 we had the most wonderful dedication service for the van, and it was my earnest hope and belief that after the Christmas and New Year break I would be privileged to start taking out this band of young Palestinian Christians. The weather during January, however, was stormy and wet, and we only had opportunity to visit one or two nearby Moslem villages.

On the Friday of the last week in January I went out in the new van to the weekly prayer meeting for missionaries held in Mr. Clarke's house. It was terrible weather, the heavens black and threatening, hailstorms, thunder and lightning, and I did not expect to find many people at the meeting. But when I got there, everything else was swallowed up in the incredible and devastating news they gave me and which I had not, till then, heard.

It had been announced in the midday radio news bulletin that in view of the increasing activities of Jewish terrorists, who were now kidnapping British officials and holding them as hostages (they had even succeeded in kidnapping a British judge in his robes while he was still sitting in the court), and their threat that they would increase their terrorist activities until Great Britain agreed to relinquish the mandate and leave the country, the government had decided to evacuate all British women and children within four days. Only nurses and women in certain indispensable positions would be allowed to remain.

All British officials after their wives and families left were to live in specially protected zones while the military combed the whole country for terrorists and put down by force all anti-government activities. They could not afford to risk having women kidnapped and held as hostages.

The whole thing seemed incredible and impossible. I simply could not believe that God would allow us to be evacuated just at this moment. He had given so many gracious promises and never had the opportunities been so great.

Not only were the Moslem villages wonderfully open to us but at last, after so many years, there was this group of Palestinian Christians ready to join in the work, and witness in this way to their own people. And the car, the new van, not quite six weeks old! What could it mean? How could God have allowed me to buy it just at this juncture if He knew that within six weeks I was to be evacuated? No, I couldn't believe that He would let me be driven out. He had intervened so many times in what had seemed miraculous ways, and now He would do the same. But He didn't.

The turmoil, agitation and upheaval of the next three days cannot be described. The whole British population was affected. Every family was perforce divided and torn asunder, and the most frantic preparations had to be made, selling furniture and closing homes, for all the men who remained had to live together in cordoned-off zones and could not stay in their own homes. For three days, like hundreds of other British women, my friends and I petitioned the authorities for permission to remain. It was all in vain. The edict was inexorable, and within four days all the British missionaries who had been doing the village and colony work were swept out of the country, though our dear fellow workers of other nationalities were, of course, allowed to remain.

On the fourth day I joined the Jerusalem convoy, and with many hundreds of other women and children, was driven down to the great camp at Sarafand.

As I alighted from the car at the reception hut, the first person I saw was my special friend, Ruth Laurence (the "Faith" of *Wayfarer in the Land).* She had just arrived in the convoy from Jaffa, and as I turned to her, almost stunned by the shock and suddenness of the affair, she exclaimed with a radiant face, "Oh, Hannah, all the promises seem contradicted, don't they? But they are not. God gave me such a lovely assurance this morning.

I was reading the story of Jeremiah going into exile, and how, even at that juncture God told him to buy a piece of land in the country he was leaving, and which was overrun by the enemy, in the sure and certain hope that God would bring His believing people back again. He will certainly bring us back too."

I can never express what those words meant to me. All the promises did indeed seem contradicted and God had not intervened to prevent our being driven forth from our land of promise, but He still remained faithful. He would bring us back in His own good time, and I left my precious six-weeks-old van behind me as a surety and pledge of this fact. He gave the van just then, that it might indeed be a pledge that we were to return, and all His promises would be fulfilled.

Next day, in a ceaseless shuttle service of R.A.F. bombers, we were flown down to Egypt and were stationed in the Maadi Camp outside Cairo. Everything possible was done for our comfort and convenience during the month we spent at Maadi, and to those of us who were kept in the peace and assurance that God would bring us back, it turned out to be a delightful holiday and enabled us to do some very pleasant sight-seeing trips in Egypt. But, naturally, so many thousands of women torn away from their husbands and many of them with no homes to go to in England were a difficult host to please and satisfy.

A great deal was written and said in criticism of the whole scheme of Operation Polly (nicknamed at once by a multitude of disgruntled women Operation Folly), but the actual truth is that it was extraordinarily well organised and made as easy and pleasant for us as possible, and as things turned out it was surely a wise proceeding. It only anticipated what would have become necessary a little later, for within less than one and a half years Britain did lay down the mandate and leave Palestine, and during those last months scarcely a week or day passed without some kind of anti-British activity and terrorism.

We remained in Maadi Camp one month and were then transferred to England and in the first week of March 1947 I found myself home in England after an absence of eight years, for during the war furlough had been impossible.

7
NOW SHALT THOU SEE WHAT I WILL DO

Some task Thou may'st set me,
Quick or hard to fret me,
Let my heart unswerving,
Trust Thee and obey.
Out of present sorrow
Springs a gladder morrow,
Love that bled to save me,
Love plans all my way.

After fifteen years of service in Palestine, this drastic uprooting and enforced return to England, with no definite prospects of ever being able to return to the Beloved Land, was one of the severest trials I had yet undergone. All the Lord's promises and assurances were connected with Palestine. For fifteen years it had been the heart and centre of all my thinking and love, and I felt I had largely lost touch with things in England, so that the uncertainty of the next few months was very hard to bear.

It would have been so different if this had been an ordinary furlough with the assurance that even after one year we would be able to return to our work. But there was no such certainty to rest on. The whole future of Palestine in that year 1947 looked dark and unpredictable in the extreme, and the little news that did come through to us was far from reassuring.

But even so I could not help marvelling, as the weeks passed, at the wonderful timing of God's plans and purposes, for I came to realise quite soon, and later far more vividly, that 1947 was the year that I would have chosen to spend in England if I had known all the facts and been able to see the future. I had not, of course, seen any of my family for eight years and, unknown to me, many changes were pending.

A few months after I reached home the way opened for my brother and his family to move to New Zealand, and if I had waited for my furlough as I was planning until 1948, I would have missed seeing them altogether. It proved, too, to be the last furlough I would spend with my dear father, for he died in January 1949.

Moreover, those quiet months of rest and furlough, including two happy months of caravan work in Cornwall with Ruth Laurence, were just what was needed after the strain of the war years and the unceasing terrorism in Palestine. They rested and restored all my energies and powers for the yet grimmer and sterner experiences which lay ahead in the unseen future. But as the summer wore on, the longing to be back in Palestine became almost intolerable, and at last, without any definite reasons for hope and encouragement, I began to believe that in some way the Lord was going to open the door and take me back. Over and over again three verses came to me.

"Now shalt thou see what I will do" (Ex. 6:1).

"Said I not unto thee, that, if thou wouldest believe, thou shouldest see the glory of God?" (John 11:40).

"I will hasten my word to perform it" (Jer. 1:12).

Now I come to one of the loveliest and most bewildering experiences of my Christian life. At the beginning of August my two most intimate friends, Beth Neatby and Ruth Laurence, came to spend a few days with me, that we might have special prayer together about the situation in Palestine, and for the few missionaries who had been able to remain there.

Each morning of their visit we drove off and settled ourselves among the trees beside a quiet little lake near my home. We read together the letters we had received from Palestine, and pondered over the news and problems, and then spread them all before the Lord. I shared with my friends the fact that I had written to the head of the Church's Ministry among the Jews in Jerusalem asking if they would be willing to apply for me to return to Jerusalem as an evangelist, if such a thing were possible. If not, I was planning to go to Syria and visit Moslem villages there until the door back into Palestine was opened.

We also read together some letters I had recently received from the matron of the C.M.J.

mission hospital in Jerusalem listing some very urgent hospital needs. These included a new doctor, another sister, and also a new housekeeper, as the housekeeper who had been with them ever since the First World War had now resigned. Most of the patients in the hospital were Jewish, and therefore Hebrew and German or Yiddish were essential, but all the domestic staff were Arabs, and therefore Arabic must be spoken too, and where they were to find an experienced housekeeper equipped with these necessary languages they could not imagine.

In Palestine people concentrated on learning either Hebrew or Arabic, according to which part of the population they worked among. Very few foreign missionaries had undertaken to learn Hebrew, believing that the determination of the Zionists to make all Jews in the country speak Hebrew was an artificial effort and would soon peter out (a mistaken conclusion which had disastrous results, for at the end of the mandate the missionary societies were left with scarcely anybody able to speak the official language of Israel).

As we talked together about the hospital's needs, this matter of the housekeeper did indeed seem rather hopeless and we did not wonder that the matron was perplexed, and wrote sadly of the special problems which anybody undertaking the job would have to face, beside and beyond the language difficulties, problems inseparable from the effort to run any institution with a staff of mixed Jewish and Arab workers at a time when there was almost a state of civil war between the two peoples, and feelings ran so high, and such bitterness was felt by both sides.

During our last prayer morning together by the lakeside, this need of a housekeeper for the English mission hospital in Jerusalem kept recurring to me in a special way. Somehow I could not get away from it, and three times over I prayed aloud that God would supply this need, adding the last time, "And, O Lord, we do feel quite sure that Thou hast somebody ready and prepared to meet this need, impossible though it looks, exactly the right person. Do make that person Thou hast chosen and prepared, hear Thy call and respond to it."

I remember opening my eyes afterwards and looking out at the quiet waters of the lake, shining through the reeds and rushes, and thinking to myself quite clearly, "Yes, God must have someone ready to meet this need. Poor soul. What a job it will be, it hardly bears thinking about. How thankful I am that I never trained for anything but evangelistic work! How I would hate to be a housekeeper! But fortunately God has other children who think quite differently, and I feel sure He must have someone, chosen and ready, somewhere, to meet this need, or He wouldn't keep pressing it on my mind."

Next morning Miss Neatby and Miss Laurence left, and by that afternoon's post I received two letters from Jerusalem. One was from the head of the mission, saying that they had already applied for permission for their own evangelist to return, and so that door was closed to me, but asking if I would consider coming out to them as housekeeper for the hospital. He understood that I had very little experience in housekeeping, and certainly it was totally different from evangelistic work, but the opportunities for evangelism in a hospital were very great, and the matron had specially suggested that I should be asked to undertake the work.

The second letter was from the matron herself, saying that for some time past she had been wanting to ask if I would help them as housekeeper at the hospital. She knew that I had enough of the requisite languages and experience in living and working among both Jews and Arabs. The departing housekeeper had trained the domestic staff admirably, and most of them had been at the hospital for many years and really only needed supervision. She felt that in this case language and understanding both Jewish and Arabic people was more important than anything else, and I would probably soon pick up the housekeeping side and get along all right.

She concluded with a loving and earnest plea that I would go and help them, and there would be no difficulty in getting permission for me to return in order to help in a hospital. Before writing to me she and two doctors had been much in prayer and they felt I was the person God meant them to ask to meet this urgent need.

If the ground had opened under my feet and swallowed me up, I could not have been more aghast and horrified. I was in the forties, and all my life I had congratulated myself that I had not trained for anything except evangelistic work, and so had avoided being pressed into secretarial, medical or educational work, which would otherwise most certainly have been the case, owing to the chronic understaffing of all mission stations.

Although it must be confessed that there were few jobs I had not helped at in an amateur capacity during times of special pressure, I had succeeded in keeping nicely out of all housekeeping responsibilities until three years previously when I had gone to share Miss Neatby's home in Beisan, a wholly Moslem town. There I had at last undertaken to do the housekeeping for our tiny, very happy little home which was run more or less on Arab lines. Superintending that sort of simple, easy-going ménage, hobnobbing with our dearly loved Arabic maid and shopping in the Arab market had been nothing but a joy, but looking after our modest little home in a remote Moslem town was as different from running a hospital institution with a big staff to supervise and to attend to the convenience and comfort of all as one could possibly imagine.

I dropped both the letters with a thrill of horror, and then began to laugh from sheer nervousness. My ever vivid imagination began to function at once, and then seemed to shy back appalled from the picture of chaos, shame and confusion which it produced. Instinctively from long habit I began speaking to the Lord and said, "What can have possessed them to suggest such a thing, Lord? How little they know me. I never heard any suggestions so preposterous."

Thus thinking in His presence His answer came to me in the usual way, for an appalling thought came to me, accompanied by the memory of placid water shining through reeds and rushes.

"But, Hannah, yesterday by the lakeside, you told Me that you were sure I had someone chosen and prepared by Me to meet this need. You trusted Me to make that person hear the call and respond to it. Well, here is the letter calling her. Not only that, you have been praying and praying that I would open the door for you to return to Palestine. You have the languages they need, and the invitation to do as much evangelistic work in the hospital as you have time for. I put it into their hearts to write and ask you. What about it?"

"But, Lord, I know absolutely nothing about housekeeping, nor of living in an institution. It would be ghastly for them! Think of the patients. Think of the staff. They must have an experienced person. It would be an awful wrong and deception to allow them to suppose for one moment that I could do the housekeeping."

"Hannah, what is the use of asking Me again and again to meet this need if you are not ready to be the answer yourself, if I ask it of you."

"But, Lord, I can't be the answer. You know I can't. It isn't unwillingness, but I don't know the first thing about housekeeping, and have never lived in an institution since I was twenty."

"I could enable you to learn."

"But it would be dreadfully wrong to deceive them, and by accepting the job lead them to suppose that I do know something about it after all."

"You can write and make the position absolutely clear. Explain about your complete inexperience and see if they still want you."

"Lord, this can't be Your voice. It simply can't be. I must be deceiving myself because I so long to get back to beloved Palestine. But I can't go back that way, Lord, it wouldn't be right. I'm sure this can't really be Your will. It is the enemy trying to deceive me. I will go to Syria as I have been planning and visit Arab villages there until the door opens back into Palestine."

But it was no good. Over and over again the memory of that quiet lakeside returned to me. I was the only one of the three who had prayed about the housekeeper, and there was that curious and unusual fact that I had felt urged to pray about it three times over, and at last had ended by saying desperately, "Lord, I am sure You have somebody already chosen and prepared. Help that chosen person to hear Thy call and respond to it." Then I remembered the special verse the Lord had given me that very morning before these letters came. It had come to me with such vivid emphasis that I had underlined and encircled it in my quiet time book.

"Thou shalt walk in the way safely, and thy foot shall not stumble. For the Lord shall be thy confidence and shall keep thy foot from being taken" (Prov. 3:23, 26).

Then surely I must act in faith in the old way, and take the first practical step towards trying to obey this extraordinary call. Then He would check and overrule if I were wrong. This was only a test perhaps. But I could not begin, after so many years, to say no to my Lord.

I cast myself on Him completely and said, "Lord, I take Thee at Thy word. I can't believe that Thou wilt leave me deceived. I trust Thee not to let my foot be taken or to allow me to be got out of Thy will in any way. If this mad idea is mad, then I trust Thee to deliver me. But if it really is Thy call, then I trust Thee to make me so sure of it that I shall go forward unafraid."

After more prayer He made it absolutely clear that at least I must set out to obey and leave Him to stop me if it was wrong. I wrote three letters, to the director in Jerusalem, to the matron, and to the head office of the mission in London, saying that I had absolutely no experience in housekeeping beyond running a small home for three or four people under very primitive conditions in an Arab town, and that I felt I was utterly unsuitable for the job. But knowing this, if they still wanted me I was willing to go out and help temporarily until they could find a really experienced and suitable housekeeper, then I would expect to be set free to return to my evangelistic work.

In the course of two or three weeks the three answers came and they all gladly accepted the offer and believed I was the one of God's choice. They expected that the permit for me to go out to the hospital in Jerusalem would be granted at once. I opened the letter from the head office at the breakfast table, skimmed through it and then exclaimed, "Oh dear, they want me, whatever shall I do?" and then sat back in my chair and laughed.

My dear father was deeply shocked. "It is nothing to laugh about," he said gravely. "It is a very serious matter, turning from such needed evangelistic work in Syria for which thou art trained and accustomed, to a purely secular task such as housekeeping in a hospital, about which thou knowest nothing and for which thou appearest to be entirely unsuited."

"Yes, I know it, father," I exclaimed penitently. "Nobody could be more unsuitable than I, and I know it is a very serious matter, but I can't help laughing. The Lord does do such funny things. This is absolutely absurd. If I don't laugh with Him about it, I can't face it. I have resisted domestic responsibilities all my life, and now in the forties He lets me in for this. I can't help seeing the funny side and you know that does make it easier. I am sure the Lord is laughing with me."

My poor father looked more shocked than ever and was silent. After breakfast at family prayers he engaged in earnest prayer for all his family and for the needs of the Lord's work in many places. But the Jerusalem hospital was left unmentioned.

It was not easy to face the reaction of my friends, for those who knew me best could not but feel I was entirely unsuited for the job. My elder sister, when I hesitantly broke the news to her, smiled a trifly sardonically. "It is difficult to picture you as housekeeper in a hospital," said she, but I blessed her from my heart when she added, "but no doubt one can learn to do anything if one puts one's whole mind to it."

I said earnestly, "I'm staking everything on the fact that if God is asking me to do this thing it is because there is some special reason or need which I know nothing about at present, but which He will make me able to fulfil. I can't believe that He will leave them dependent upon me as a housekeeper very long, but meanwhile I do mean to put my whole heart into it, and really enjoy doing it. For it is misery to do God's work grudgingly."

My little quiet time books are full of the inner struggle and doubts and fears of those weeks, and I have copied one extract as a sample of how the Lord enabled me to understand and really believe that this astonishing thing was His will.

8th August, 1947.

"Faithful is He that calleth you, Who also will do it" (I Thess. 5:24).

I had a very restless night, tossing about, thinking of the letter I wrote yesterday offering myself as an inexperienced, temporary housekeeper for the Jerusalem hospital. How shall I manage if they accept the offer? I must really be turning queer in the head. I tried to picture it, and felt awful. What can be happening to me but middle-aged madness, turning away from the village work I have done for so many years, to a housekeeping job in a hospital, when I haven't the ghost of a notion how to begin such work.

I was so miserable and sleepless, at last I turned on the light and opened *Daily Light* and read, "The path of the just is as a shining light, which shineth more and more until the perfect day" (Prov. 4:18).

Beside me lay my little Bible, still open at the verse He has given me so often lately, "Faithful is He that calleth you, Who also will do it" (I Thess. 5:24). This verse just spoke to my need, as does "The Lord shall be thy confidence and shall keep thy foot from being taken" (Prov. 3:26). I can and will trust my Lord. He will intervene if I am wrong over this matter, and if it is His will for me and His call, then He will do everything Himself and make me able to go through with it to His glory.

For weeks past He has been saying to me, "Thou shalt not be put to shame. Now shalt thou see what I will do."

Well, the Levites were to lead the way praising and singing, and the battle was the Lord's. But O my Lord, my dear Lord, what scarecrows the devil has planted all over this new field that lies ahead.

Just three weeks later I returned to the Holy Land, flying there on the wings of the morning. One moment we were still over the blue Mediterranean, the next we had passed above the white beach and the plane was circling low over the orange groves on the Plain of Sharon, with the mountains of Judea in the hazy distance. So down to Lydda

Airport—and the exile was home again.

How can I decribe the mingled feelings of exultant joy and gratitude which flooded one half of my heart, and the dread and shrinking in the other? I, the exile, was home again in the land I loved best on earth, but I realised that incredible as it seemed, the terrifying fact remained, I was returning as housekeeper to the hospital and had all the ordeal before me of either being transformed by the grace of God into what I felt I could never become, or else of being ashamed and confounded by turning out a ghastly failure. But as I drove up the mountain road to Jerusalem, joy and gratitude cast out everything else and I found myself singing in my heart Psalm 126.

"When the Lord turned again the captivity of Zion, we were like them that dream. Then was our mouth filled with laughter and our tongue with singing, then said they . . . The Lord hath done great things for us whereof we are glad . . . They that sow in tears shall reap in joy. He that goeth forth and weepeth, bearing precious seed, shall doubtless come again with rejoicing, bringing his sheaves with him."

I remembered the last time that I had passed along that road when all the promises seemed contradicted and I was being driven out of the Land of Promise. Now God had brought me back again, seven months later. How could I ever suppose that He would not be just as faithful in the future. He Who had given this new call was faithful, and had promised to perform it for me.

Now comes the really extraordinary part. The retiring housekeeper stayed for six weeks longer, showing me the ropes and helping me to get accustomed to my new job, and on the very day that she left and the keys were handed over to me, partition was announced and the Jews and Arabs began the last desperate phase of their long struggle. Great Britain then declared her intention of giving up the mandate within six months. Then it began to become clear in the most extraordinary way why God had called me to accept the hospital job just at that identical moment.

Within one month of the time that I was left in charge as housekeeper, it became evident that the political situation in the country and the certainty of war between the Arabs and Jews, as soon as the mandate ended, would make it necessary to close the mission hospital and all other mission institutions.

A few hours after partition was announced Jerusalem was split into two sectors, Arab and Jewish. Our hospital was in the Jewish sector, but all the domestic staff were Arabic, and by December we realised that none of them would be able to remain. The Jewish nurses, on the other hand, were all called up to join Jewish hospitals and prepare for the great struggle ahead when war started. Then as the hospital was situated in Jewish territory, it was completely cut off from all its old sources of supply in the Arab market.

From the very first day that I took over the housekeeping, I had, personally, to fetch in my precious God-given van every crumb of food that we ate. The hospital itself did not possess a car, but I went daily in my commercial van out of the Jewish into the Arab area in order to buy all our supplies. This was only possible because I was a Britisher and so was granted permission to pass through the British Zone which acted as a sort of buffer state between the two belligerent areas. As soon as the mandate ended, this buffer state would of course cease to exist and the Jewish half of Jerusalem would be in a state of complete siege as it was cut off from all the rest of the Jewish land in the country.

It became obvious therefore that the best way to continue our witness to the Jewish people would be to hand the hospital over to them, at least for the duration of the war, for the mission could no longer staff it, and the splendidly equipped Jewish hospital on Mount Scopus was quite out of their reach in the Arab sector.

I have written about these things in *Watchmen on the Walls,* but mention them again here in order to show the extraordinary way in which God had worked. For here was a special job for me to do, for which there was no one else available.

How I thanked God that He had led me to buy a van and not a saloon car, for it was able to hold such things as sacks of grain, rice, flour, and tins of kerosene, which could never have been got into a small saloon car. So few people at that time did possess cars, and I with the van and free permission to pass through the British Zone from area to area, was able to fetch and carry, not only for the hospital but for many other missionary and Christian groups. For there was no transport between the two areas, and those who had to move out of one into the other could find no means of getting their belongings moved.

The well trained domestic staff at the hospital carried on during those emergency months, very largely on their own, while my time was spent in moving goods and chattels, shopping, conveying Arabs out of the Jewish area and stores in from the Arab area, smuggling Hebrew Christians to places of safety (how I blessed the absence of windows in the back of the van) and taking workers to and fro between the mission premises in both areas.

Eventually my precious van was almost the only non-military and non-police car still able to pass to and fro between the zones, and God kept this door open in a most wonderful way, up till the last ten minutes of the mandate, and I passed through the neutral zone for the last time just before the British left and the two opposing armies rushed to take possession. Thus it was possible to lay in stores for the approaching siege, not just for the two C.M.J. missionaries and myself who planned to remain in the beseiged area but also to help stock the storerooms of other missionaries who expected to remain.

What a joy and privilege it was! The daily trips, especially towards the end, had sometimes to be taken under quite heavy fire. I would not write about these things if it were not for the joy of testifying that the Lord Jesus is able, in such times of crisis, to overcome our natural fears and give such a glorious realisation of His presence that everything else is swallowed up.

Thus God demonstrated again, in this striking way, how absolutely safe it had been to trust Him in what had looked so crazy a proceeding, and to step out in blind obedience. There had indeed been a special need and a special work to do, and one for which my past training in travelling about the country during the riots helped to fit me. Then too, how marvellous it was that when the hospital closed down, I was on the spot and was permitted with the other two C.M.J. missionaries to stay on the mission compound and to have the unspeakable privilege of remaining in Jewish Jerusalem all through the siege.

And when the war was over and an armistice in force, there I was in the new state of Israel, needing no further permission to remain, with none of the problems and perplexities connected with getting a permit to return, and able within a few months to restart the work to which the van had been dedicated.

How precious God's thoughts are! How far past finding out! How utterly safe it is to trust Him if only we are willing to obey and leave all the responsibility to Him. The verse which seems to sum up perfectly the whole strange experience and its wonderful outcome is Isaiah 28:29. "This also cometh forth from the Lord of Hosts, Who is wonderful in counsel and excellent in working."

How truly and joyfully I can testify

as I look back over my path of life "faithful is He that calleth you, Who also will do it."

"I have led thee in right paths."

Amen, Lord. Yes, ever since that radiant day when I knelt beside my bed at Keswick and Thou didst take me to be Thine own, Thy grace has been sufficient for me, and Thou hast enabled poor Miss Much-Afraid to keep following. No giant has been allowed to turn her back, no evil to come nigh her dwelling. And oh how gladly and thankfully she says to Thee again today,

Bond that cannot alter,
Though the flesh may falter,
In Thy face I've looked, Lord,
Laid my hand in Thine.

Owned Thy claims upon me,
Thou my Master only,
I Thy slave forever,
Nothing henceforth mine.

8
SOME PRACTICAL POINTS

When I first emerged from the amazing and shattering crisis of becoming a Christian, I had no idea that I would meet other sincere Christians who would think it strange, indeed almost presumptuous, to be sure that God is ready and able to speak to us as plainly as our friends do, and to give clear guidance when we seek it from Him, making us so unmistakably sure of His will that, if necessary, we will attempt things which to other people look strange, or ridiculous, and perhaps in some cases crazy.

The idea of being guided only by circumstances, as one prayed to be helped to do His will and to make decisions in the most sensible way, never occurred to me. I never doubted that all true Christians heard His voice (in the Scriptural sense) in exactly the same way as did the prophets and the Spirit-led men in the Bible.

For example, it never seemed strange to me to read over and over again: "The word of the Lord came to . . . ," or "The Holy Spirit said . . . ," for that was exactly the utterly amazing but joyful and transforming experience that was mine—I to whom God had been so inconceivable and unreal. Neither did it ever occur to me that the people in the Bible, except when they had visions, were accustomed to hear an actual audible voice speaking to them. I took it for granted that they received the word of the Lord in the same way that present day Christians do, and not by means of any special mystical faculty.

The only difference, it seemed to me, between the word of the Lord coming to a prophet of old was a difference in degree, due to greater spiritual enlightenment, because through long or faithful practice they had developed the hearing heart to a greater degree than others. Thus they could be trusted with far greater and more important messages than we beginners.

Of course I do not mean that the kind of messages which God spoke at special times to His servants the prophets are given to all His people. For it is clear that there have been certain men, and sometimes women, chosen and set apart by God to receive special messages for their nation, or for the whole world, at certain great crises in history. Such people were commanded to utter solemn warnings, and they were often given supernatural understanding and vision of future events.

God does not choose to make all His people prophets in that sense. We are clearly told that there are diversities of gifts and callings (I Cor. 12) and that the Holy Spirit Who develops in us the hearing heart calls some to be sent ones, others preachers, and others evangelists, pastors, teachers, healers, and some prophets.

But it did seem perfectly natural to suppose from the teaching in the Bible and our Lord's own sayings that all heard His voice in the same way, and that there were not some endowed with a special and mysterious faculty for hearing which was not granted to others. The least child of God can hear in the same way, and be sure that it is the voice of God speaking to him, as any holy man of old, provided he knows and practises the one principle by which the spirit of man can develop a hearing faculty.

Again, this does not mean that we shall ever become infallible or that all our thoughts at all times will be from God. Far from it, especially, of course, at the beginning of our Christian experience. In matters of Christian truth and understanding of the Scriptures, we learn slowly and by stages; a hearing heart, too, may in some cases develop more quickly than a seeing understanding. Every new obedience, however, leads to a fuller understanding, but is always accompanied by an ever increasing realisation that there is infinitely more beyond our present ability to comprehend, and that there is an ever present danger of becoming self-confident and being dogmatic to others. Nothing deafens a hearing heart more quickly than unwillingness to keep open to further light.

The great principle of the hearing heart is that we become as little children, utterly dependent and always ready to obey. We have to learn to obey His guidance in small personal matters, before we can receive and understand more of His will and purposes.

But we must hear, or how can God teach us? And learning to hear and to understand and to obey is the most vital thing in Christian experience. It always came as an immense surprise to me to hear other Christians say, as some did, "How can you be sure? Beware of presumption. You are just imagining your guidance." (That suggestion, by the way, will generally present itself to one's own mind, and is a very useful safeguard, making one very dependent and earnestly desirous of further assurance from the Lord.

The very fact that spiritual hearing can so easily be confused with imagination is a great safeguard against spiritual pride and ought to develop in us holy cautiousness and humble dependence. But to insist that unusual guidance is only imagination, and that real guidance is really using one's common sense, did seem to me extraordinary. For most of the guidance which came to me in those early years did not make common sense at all, and generally involved me in the risk of appearing an absolute fool in the eyes of others. Of course, common sense and all one's intellectual faculties, as well as the experience and wisdom of others, are all part of the wonderful equipment and means by which God does reveal to us His will.

One point that I would like to emphasise is that just as some people find great help through outward symbols (while others are hindered by them) I, and many others, do find that God clarifies the mind and helps towards the realisation of His wishes and guidance, as questions and problems are put down on paper. Often even as I express the question on paper, the very fact of clarifying the problem or need in my own thoughts enables me to see the true answer and solution to the problem. For others, of course, this seems an extraordinary, unnecessary and very peculiar habit which would not help them at all. But I find my quiet time notebooks indispensable, helping me to clarify my thoughts ready for His use, and then recording the answers He gives so that they are not forgotten or overlooked.

Some Christians that I met even went so far as to say that to expect to get guidance from God about every tiny detail of our daily lives was not only nonsense and neglect of the common sense which He has given us but was even irreverent. This always mystified me. It just didn't fit in with one's personal radiant and yet awe-inspiring experience.

To go to spiritual advisers and mature Christians is a most lovely Christian privilege and help, if you live in a place where they are available. But what are you to do, for instance, if you are the only Christian in some irreligious place, or if God sends you to some lonely out-station on the mission field, where you have to become spiritual adviser to others, and you have never developed the hearing heart and cannot recognise your Lord's voice, thus enabling you to go unhesitatingly forward even when you cannot see the next step. What human being can ever enable a shrinking soul to have the faith which steps on the seeming abyss, and finds the Rock beneath? Only God can.

So in loving sympathy and understanding with all who long to find a deeper reality in their spiritual life and to know what it is to be drawn into intimate, daily communion and fellowhip with the Lord and Saviour Himself, I would joyfully and humbly share these experiences, praying that He Who is so real and so full of understanding love will use them to help others into the radiant happiness of those who can say,

> I have seen the face of Jesus,
> Tell me nought of earth beside,
> I have heard the voice of Jesus,
> And my soul is satisfied.